LONE WOLF

SHIFTERS UNBOUND

JENNIFER ASHLEY

JA / AG PUBLISHING

CHAPTER ONE

W hoa there, little lady."

Maria stopped, scrabbling to hang on to the tray loaded with beer bottles and glasses, to find the asshat who'd been bugging her all night standing in front of her. He was human, annoying, and in the Shifter bar for kicks.

Maria had labeled him *asshat* the second he'd walked in the door, for two reasons. First, he'd strolled in with his friends in his greasy jeans and baseball cap, unshaved whiskers, and attitude. He was human, he was superior—he thought—over these Shifters and the little human Maria who was there to serve him.

Second, Maria called him *asshat,* because Ellison liked that word, and she liked Ellison.

"You bringing those to my table?" the man said, raising his voice over the rollicking country song playing on the old-fashioned jukebox. "None of that watery crap, right?"

"Your order's coming," Maria said with cool dignity. "This is for them." She jerked her chin at a cluster of Lupine

Shifters in the corner, one family—brothers, sisters, father, and mother, all having a good time.

"Don't think so. We're tired of waiting. Take it to our table."

Maria stood her ground. "Not yet."

"You talking back to me, bitch? Someone needs to teach you a lesson."

With a practiced hand, the man banged the tray upward from the bottom. Maria tried to hang on to it, but the tray became a vertical plane, and bottles and glasses slid off to land in a spectacular crash on the floor. Beer fountained over Maria's black leggings, glass skittering past her sneakers. The asshat danced back, laughing ...

Right into a tall Shifter in jeans and a button-down shirt, with honey-colored hair, wolf-gray eyes, and a body that bulked above the human man's. His large hand, tanned by the sun, landed on the human's shoulder.

The music from the jukebox ran down, and the Shifter's slow drawl sounded over the last strains. "I think you need to apologize to the lady, son."

Ellison's grip on the man's shoulder looked loose and relaxed, but Maria saw the asshat flinch, his pale eyes widening. "Stupid clumsy bitch dropped beer all over me."

Ellison's fingers tightened. "Wrong answer," he said in his fine baritone. "You go over to the bar and pay for what was on that tray, then you and your friends get on out of here."

"Screw you. I ain't paying for that. She dropped it. Take it out of her paycheck."

His stupid trick hadn't angered Maria much, but his last words made her fury rise. She needed every penny of her paycheck and her tips for the goal she'd determined as soon as she'd moved back to the Austin Shiftertown six months ago. Every day she worked for it, saving everything she could, so that one day, she'd not have to put up with asshats like this, or live on the charity of the Shifters who'd rescued her.

Another Shifter, a scary-looking Feline with a shaved head and body full of tattoos, was already coming up behind Ellison. His name was Spike, and when Maria had first seen him, when she'd arrived in Shiftertown scared and broken, she'd wanted to run the other way.

Asshat didn't notice him, and he didn't notice the tall, black-haired, blue-eyed Shifter who ran the place coming up behind Spike. The man *did* see the Shifter Maria sensed behind her—Ronan, a giant of a man who could turn into a Kodiak bear. Hard to miss Ronan.

The human man paled. Liam Morrissey, the black-haired Shifter, stepped into the man's line of sight. Liam flashed his smile that could melt paint off a building, and the asshat looked uncertain.

Shifters did that—they charmed and terrified you at the same time. They could gaze at their prey with half-closed eyes, like animals dozing in the sun. The next moment, they'd be awake, alert, focused right on you, while your animal brain yelled at you to run, run, run ...

Shifters might wear Collars, but they weren't tame, and they sure as hell weren't safe.

"Now then, lad." Liam moved around the man with his lanky grace and stopped a foot in front of Maria and a little to her right.

This forced the human man to turn slightly, moving his line of attack away from Maria. Ellison adjusted so that he was now half behind the human and half on his left side, a position from which he could grab said man if he tried to go for Maria. Spike and Ronan moved in to cover any remaining gaps in the circle.

Maria had seen the same tactics during her three years of absolute terror living with a pack of feral Shifters. No, not *living* with them. They'd stolen her from her family and imprisoned her in a warehouse basement with other females.

She'd watched those Shifters form similar circles around intruders or with dissidents within their own pack. They'd surround the victim, not threatening, not attacking. Just intimidating.

Shifters had intimidation down to an art. The Shifters in Mexico had finished their circle of fear by killing the intruders and the dissidents. Maria had never seen the Austin Shifters kill anyone, and they wore Collars made to shock them if they grew violent, but she knew the potential for destruction was there.

Something deep in the asshat's drunken brain knew it too, but he tried to brazen it out. "I'm not paying for shit."

"Nor will you be," Liam said smoothly. His Irish lilt was musical and deep, despite twenty and more years living in Texas. "You'll leave this bar on the moment, and you won't be coming back again. Not ever, I'm thinking."

He smiled when he said it—the smile of a lion who knows the gazelle is within paw's reach. Didn't hurt the lion to be nice to the gazelle.

"You don't own this bar, you piece of Shifter turd," the man said. "You can't throw me out, or my friends."

"It looks like your friends have already left. Fine men they are for deserting you, aren't they?"

The man looked around, blinking when he realized he stood alone, surrounded by Shifters. His friends, who'd been loud and obnoxious in the corner, had quietly walked out when Ronan had left his post.

"Ellison," Liam said, looking over the asshat's head. "See that he gets out, will you? I'll put you in charge of his safety. Spike, go with him."

Ellison's grin flashed. It was a wolf's grin, matching the large gray wolf Ellison became when he shifted. His was a fine-looking beast, with silver gray fur that shone in the moonlight, and a long-legged grace that went with his strong face.

"I'd be happy to." Ellison returned his hand to the human's shoulder. No mistaking the flinch that time. "This way, son."

"Stop calling me *son*."

Ellison laughed, his strong accent booming through the room as he said, "Hey there, Ronan. Why don't you back off and let the man through?"

Ronan—who, Maria had come to know, was one of the gentlest guys in Shiftertown—instead moved to block the doorway, folded his arms, and looked mean. Seven feet tall, he made a formidable barrier, and the rumbling in his throat became a deep, vibrating growl.

"Come on now, Ronan," Ellison said. "Liam says we got to let the man go."

Ronan glared down at the asshat, whose face was now shining with sweat.

Spike—the tall, tattooed biker-looking Shifter—moved past Ellison and leaned his hand on the doorframe. As though he and Ronan went through an unspoken conversation, Ronan finally nodded and turned sideways in the doorway to let Ellison and the man pass.

Ellison, hand on the man's shoulder, steered him between Spike and Ronan. Ronan left barely enough room for them to squeeze through into the glaring lights of the parking lot.

Maria went to the doorway to watch, as did every other Shifter in the bar. Ellison turned the man loose at the edge of the parking lot, halting as the man jogged across the dark street and got himself into a pickup.

"Y'all *don't* come back, now," Ellison called after him. "Hear?"

The truck roared to life. The man peeled out onto the quiet road, squealed around the corner, and was gone.

Ronan laughed, the loud sound filling the bar. Ellison strolled back inside and high-fived first Ronan then Spike. Ellison's laugh joined Ronan's in loud, rich warmth, and Spike added his grin. Liam stood back and watched the three with a fond look an older brother might give mischievous siblings.

Ellison let out a whoop. "Good fun, Liam. You all right, Maria?"

His cowboy boots crunched on the glass in the middle of the room. Maria, shaking from anger, fear, and watching Ellison's eyes soften to warm gray as he looked at her, lost her temper.

The human man had unnerved her, and the Shifters surrounding him like stalking beasts had reminded her too strongly of the Shifters who'd held her captive. Shifters were Shifters, and Maria would never be safe.

She swept a shaking finger and a scowl around the four

men, ending at Ellison. "*Locos.* You'll bring the police in here, and then they'll close the bar, and I won't have a job. I *need* this job."

She ended shouting up at Ellison, who blinked his gray eyes then turned up his grin. "Now, sweetheart, it was good fun, and that asshat is too scared to do anything to retaliate. He's gone."

"I could have taken care of him, until you had to step in with all your muscles."

No, no, the term was *muscle in.* That's what they said on TV shows—Maria was learning all her American slang from television.

Ellison started laughing again. "Yeah, me and my muscles to the rescue. Don't leave out Ronan's. His are pretty hefty."

"You gobshite," Maria snapped. Liam was also teaching Maria slang. She retrieved the tray from the floor and held it up like a weapon. "If he tells the owner I made trouble, who will get fired? *Me.* You don't even work here."

"Now, honey ... "

Said in Ellison's deep voice, the endearment made Maria warm inside, threatening to assuage her anger. Which was why she raised the tray and started for him.

Liam's big hand yanked the tray from her hands. "Take a break, child."

Maria opened her mouth to let her hot temper have its way, but one look in Liam's eyes made her close it again. "I don't need a break," she said. "I'll clean this up and get back to work."

"I'll be cleaning it up," Liam said. He jerked his thumb at the office door in the dark rear of the bar. "You. Break. Now."

No one argued with Liam. Not for long. At least, no one but his wife, his brother, his father, his nephew, and now his little girl, who couldn't even talk yet. Maria raised her chin, turned her back on the Shifters, walked past Ellison, shoes crunching broken glass, and slammed her way into the empty office.

———

ELLISON STARTED AFTER HER AND FOUND LIAM IN HIS way. "Let her go," Liam said in his quiet voice. "Give the lass time to catch her breath."

Ellison eyed the office door between him and Maria, a barrier he needed to break down. That Liam formed another barrier made him growl in irritation.

Maria lived in Shiftertown under the Morrisseys' protection, staying in Liam's brother Sean's house. She'd been brought here by Liam's dad a year ago after she'd been rescued from feral Shifters. She'd then gone to stay with her brother, who lived way out in El Paso and who had sponsored her to get her a visa. But the brother had made it clear that he, like her parents, considered Maria ruined goods and a disgrace to the family.

Maria had returned to Shiftertown after six months, and Liam made sure she got hired on at the bar he managed. In her off time, Maria cleaned houses, ran errands, and looked after cubs for Shifters who paid her. She worked nonstop, her energy amazing. Ellison's sister had said, with a laugh, that Maria could be a Shifter with stamina like that.

Liam brought out a broom from behind the bar, then the great alpha Feline, leader of his pride, his clan, and all of

Shiftertown, went to work sweeping up the glass. Spike, one of the most formidable fighters in Shiftertown, grabbed a mop and started helping him.

Another Lupine stopped next to Ellison—Broderick, who was in the second wolf pack in Shiftertown. Ellison's pack was very small. Most of his clan had died out in the wild, their immediate family going just before Shifters took the Collar, leaving Ellison, his sister, and his sister's tiny cubs alone. Shiftertown had been good to them, letting the boys, Jackson and Will, grow up unharmed.

"She's ripe," Broderick said. He was watching the office door, behind which Maria rested, his gray eyes intense.

Ellison tightened, the wolf in him tense, readying itself to take down a rival. Ellison kept his voice mild when he said, "I think she smells pretty good."

"I mean she needs to be mated. Soon. Now."

"I know what you meant." *Asshole.* "But she's off-limits." Liam and Dylan had made that clear. "To you, to me, to all Shifters."

"That's bullshit. This is a Shiftertown full of mateless Shifters. And she's fair game."

Ellison didn't bother to answer. *Fair game* was a female without a mate, a clan, a pack or pride. A female whose mate had died and who had no family to return to was considered fair game, as was a female stolen from another clan. Unmated, unprotected. *Shifter leavings* was another term Ellison had heard.

Maria wasn't quite the same. First, she was human, and second, she was definitely under Morrissey protection.

Good thing she was. As soon as Maria had returned to Shiftertown, intending to stay a while, male Shifters had started sniffing around. Maria had formerly been mated to a Shifter, she smelled of Shifters, and Shifters were desperate for mates.

Including Ellison.

"She's off-limits," Ellison repeated with a growl.

Broderick laughed. He was tall and rangy, with a buzz cut and white gray eyes. "And don't you just hate that?"

Ellison did. Maria was lovely, with her black hair, red mouth, and lush hips outlined by the black leggings she wore to waitress, but Ellison saw the bleakness in her eyes. Her life had been destroyed by Shifters, and she was hurt, and she grieved.

He eyed the blank panel of the closed door, knowing Maria was hurting behind it. He wanted to go to her, put his arms around her, and say, *Hey, sweetheart, it will be all right. I'll fix everything for you.*

But he knew he couldn't. The Shifters who'd captured Maria had sequestered her—Shifters in the wild in ancient times had locked their females away from all others in the same way. She'd been imprisoned against her will, hurt, terrified—nothing that would heal easily, if ever. The best Ellison could do right now was turn Broderick away from the door and let Maria have some peace.

"Ellison." Annie, another waitress, passed Ellison with a tray of drinks to replace the one Maria had lost. "You have a phone call."

Ellison put his hand on the cell phone in his pocket, but it was silent. At the bar, the human bartender briefly held up the house phone, then set it down to pour the next drink.

Ellison didn't want to take his eyes off Broderick, but he

knew that neither Liam nor Spike would let anyone into the office with Maria, especially Broderick.

Ellison made his way to the phone, thanked the bartender, and picked up the receiver, wondering who'd call the bar, not his cell phone.

"Yeah?" he drawled.

"Ellison?" the breathless voice of one of his nephews came to him. "You need to get back here. It's Mom. She's gone again."

CHAPTER TWO

Ellison tore away from the bar and sprinted out into the darkness, his nephew's words pounding through his head. The wolf in him told him he could move faster in animal form, but Ellison didn't want to lose precious minutes stopping to undress and shift.

He ran up the porch steps of his house to find all the lights on inside. Jackson, the older of his nephews, met him at the door.

"We tried to stop her," Jackson said, panicked. "But you know what happens."

"Tell Andrea to come over," Ellison said, pushing past him. Andrea, a wolf Shifter who lived in the house across the street, was a healer. They might need her.

Ellison raced down the hall in the one-story bungalow to his sister's bedroom, finding his second nephew, Will, waiting anxiously in the doorway. Will, twenty-four, the youngest of Denise's cubs, had tears in his gray eyes.

"She's bad this time."

Ellison paused to put his hands on Will's shoulders. "Jackson's getting Andrea over here to help. Don't worry."

Will returned the clasp, slightly comforted by Ellison's touch, but he didn't relax.

Ellison stepped into Deni's bedroom. In the middle of it, facing him, was a huge gray wolf with murder in her eyes.

Deni wasn't as large as Ellison, being female and about forty years younger, but she was a Shifter, and that made her powerful. She snarled at Ellison, no recognition in her expression.

Deni's room was a wreck—furniture overturned, clothing shredded on the floor. The window blind had been half ripped down, the slats tangled as though an animal had seen something through them and had gone for the window, not caring that the blind was in the way.

Deni sniffed, smelling Ellison fresh from the bar, and then snarled again, ears flattening on her head. The Collar around her neck emitted several sparks.

Ellison carefully didn't move. He was Deni's alpha, leader of their tiny pack. Though it broke his heart to see her like this, at the moment he needed to be less worried brother and more alpha wolf.

"Den." He made his voice firm but not harsh.

Deni growled right through the word, an arc of electricity running around her Collar. Ever since whatever foul bastard had run her down on her motorcycle and left her mangled and half-dead, Deni had been having episodes of forgetting who she was, who Ellison was, who her own cubs were.

Each time this happened, she reverted into her wolf and stayed there—threatening like a cornered animal.

Deni's body had healed fairly quickly—Shifters had incredible metabolisms that closed wounds swiftly. Plus, they had Andrea—half Shifter, half Fae—who had Fae healing magic, made greater when she channeled it through her mate, Sean, the Shiftertown Guardian. They'd brought Deni back from death and thought all was well.

Then had come the first episode of Deni's brain more or less shutting off and making her forget everything she was. Human doctors couldn't find anything wrong with her, and Andrea couldn't help.

What Deni needed was a Shifter healer—one stronger than Andrea, well versed in ailments from which Shifters could suffer. The trouble was, Shifter healers weren't thick on the ground, if any even existed these days, and Deni was sick *now*.

"Deni," Ellison said again, making his voice hard with command. "It's Ellison."

Deni snarled one last time, then attacked.

Ellison blocked her leap with arms folded to protect his face. He took the brunt of her weight, sparks from her Collar dancing across his skin, and they went backward together.

Ellison's heightened Shifter senses scented his nephews in the hall, scared and unhappy. He smelled Deni, enraged and terrified, as her wolf untangled herself from him, whirled, and leapt at him again.

Ellison caught her in his arms this time and swung around with her, using the momentum of her impact to toss her away across the room. Deni smashed into a wall, the thud of the contact lost in her growls. She came to her feet with terrible swiftness, her eyes red with rage, her gray coat dusted with plaster that had cracked off the wall.

Deni went for Ellison again, fangs bared. The Collar was taking its toll on her—Deni was a little slower this time, the impact not as strong. Ellison saw pain in her eyes as she landed on him.

This time she clung on with her claws, her jaws snapping at his neck. Ellison changed under her grip, his favorite black cowboy shirt ripping as his massive wolf shoulders burst through it.

His own Collar sparked as he caught Deni's muzzle with his mouth, now a wolf's mouth, turning aside her deadly bite.

Ellison tasted her blood, the blood of his pack, and his feral rage ignited. No wolf attacked the alpha and lived.

The human part inside him knew that this was his sister, lashing out, scared. The wolf in him said it was one of the pack, hurt yes, but she needed to be subdued.

Both entities wove together and knew what to do. Ellison released Deni's muzzle and went for her throat, locking his teeth around loose fur. Deni howled, her Collar sparking wildly as she shook her head to try to tear free.

Ellison held on tighter, carefully not letting his teeth break her skin. He put his large paw on her head and used his weight to bear her to the floor. He landed on top of her, his wolf big enough to cover her and keep her down.

He heard the distinctive footsteps of Andrea and then Glory, Dylan's mate, following his nephews—Andrea sure-footed and graceful, like her wolf, Glory with the click-click of impossibly high heels.

Deni howled, still fighting, but Ellison's hold was strong. Deni growled and snarled, terrified, not understanding.

"I can tranq her," Glory said.

Ellison didn't want Deni tranqed. She'd been given

drugs and sedatives, poked and prodded. She didn't need another round of tranquilizers that would leave her groggy and afraid.

But they might not have a choice. Deni was still fighting, weakening, but fighting. She still didn't know who Ellison was—she was lost and scared, afraid to yield to the wolf who pinned her. In the wild, Ellison would have had every right to kill her for the safety of the pack. Deni's wolf, by the look in her eyes, somehow sensed this.

"Mom," Jackson said, voice thick with tears. "Mom, try. Please."

Deni snarled again, trying to dislodge Ellison. Her Collar gave her a barrage of shocks, which shocked Ellison at the same time, hot bites of pain.

Ellison growled, a long, low sound. *Stop. I'm your brother. Those are your cubs. Come* on, *Den.*

Deni snarled again, then she blinked once, twice, and her eyes cleared. She drew a breath through her wolf muzzle, and her Collar went silent.

Ellison snatched his teeth away from her throat as Deni shifted to human, lifting himself away from her before he could hurt her. Tears filled Deni's eyes. "Jackson?"

"Mom."

Jackson fell on his knees beside Deni as Ellison shifted back to his human form. Ellison's arms went around his sister, and she relaxed into his strong embrace.

Ellison kissed her hair, holding her, rocking her. Deni reached for Jackson, who came into the embrace with them, her son openly crying. Will knelt on Deni's other side, sliding his arms around his mother's waist.

Ellison didn't get up, knowing that Deni needed his

comfort, his forgiveness, his understanding. Her cubs gave her love, and Ellison gave her strength.

"So," Glory said. Ellison heard the butt of the tranquilizer rifle click softly on the floor. "We won't be needing the tranq, then."

"No," Andrea said. "Just me."

She came to kneel beside Ellison, careful not to break the family huddle. Ellison couldn't have let Deni go for anything right now, in any case. Andrea reached between them, laid her hand on Deni's forearm, and let her healing magic trickle into Deni to soothe her better than any man-made tranquilizer ever could.

Ellison felt the small pulse of magic flowing into him through Deni. Though Glory was the leader of the rival Lupine pack in this Shiftertown—Broderick's pack—and Andrea her niece, Ellison had nothing but gratitude for them.

———

Maria finished her shift without any more asshats harassing her, or drinks spilling, or glasses breaking.

Liam had cleaned up the mess by the time she emerged from his office, the floor pristinely clean. He said nothing to her about the incident, only winked at her as she walked back to the bar to fill her next order. The rest of the Shifters had gone back to drinking, laughing, and talking, the excitement over.

Maria's shift that night finished before the bar closed. She let Ronan walk her partway home, but he had to get back to help Liam close, and she told him to go. Shiftertown lay before her, with its small bungalows and neat yards, quiet under the cool of the night. Summer would hit soon, with sticky weather that only Austin and its river and creeks could bring.

Ellison had gone before Maria emerged from the office, long gone, Spike told her. Jackson had called, and Ellison had raced home.

Spike, a man of few words, of course hadn't been that effusive. What he'd said was: "Ellison went. Jackson called. While ago."

Maria knew why. Poor Deni, and her poor sons. Jackson and Will were grown men in human terms but still considered cubs to Shifters.

She hoped everything was all right. She'd have to visit Deni tomorrow if all was well, maybe cook her something. Buñuelos. Deni liked those, and they were fairly easy to put together. Sean always kept flour, sugar, and honey around for making his pancakes, and never minded when Maria used the ingredients. Maria helped pay for groceries with her tips from the bar, in any case.

Her tips had been pretty good tonight. Maria's pockets were full of coins and bills, more for her jar of savings.

A shadow rose beside her, and a Shifter fell into step with her. "I liked how you stood up to that human," the Lupine called Broderick said. "Took guts."

"Thank you." Maria kept walking, though her calm had shattered again. Broderick liked to follow her home, to walk to close to her. Though he'd never done anything inappropriate in Shifter terms, he violated her personal space all the time, doing everything but rubbing against her.

"No one would do that to you if you had a mate," Broderick said.

His constant argument. "I don't want a mate," Maria said quickly. She'd been mate-claimed by one of the Lupines in Miguel's Shifter pack, and at first, she'd been stupidly enchanted with Luis, which was how she'd been stolen from home in the first place. She'd learned quickly about the things Miguel expected from females brought in by his feral males.

At first, Maria had blamed herself for falling for tall, handsome Luis, but she knew now that if she hadn't have run away with Luis willingly, he'd have kidnapped her. Miguel and his Shifters had dominated Maria's little town, and there had been nothing her family or any of the other townspeople could do.

"Yeah, you keep going on that you don't want anything to do with Shifters," Broderick said. "But you live here, honey. You can't be wriggling your ass at us and then telling us we can't have any. Not when male Shifters are dying to mate."

Maria shivered, and not from the breeze. She was too alone out here, the first houses of Shiftertown half a block away. If she tried to run, Broderick would be on her before she took two steps.

"Maybe someday," Maria said. But not if she could help it. She had her plan, and she would be free.

"Maybe *now*." Broderick grabbed her arm and leaned close, breathing into her face. Maria cringed back from the scent of stale beer. "Maria Ortega, I mate-claim you under the light of the mother goddess."

Maria tried to break free, but his hand was strong.

"There's no moon tonight, and you have to do it in front of witnesses." She knew that much.

Broderick's grip bore down. "Then let's go find us some witnesses."

"Here's one," came a male growl.

Ellison appeared out of nowhere, a mass in the dark, reaching for Broderick. Ellison's face was bruised, as though he'd been fighting, his hair a mess. He clamped one hand around Broderick's neck and yanked him away from Maria.

"You heard me," Broderick managed to say, even with Ellison's fingers digging into his throat. "I claim this female in front of a witness."

Ellison snarled, his eyes tinged with red. "Then I Challenge."

CHAPTER THREE

Ellison smelled Maria's fear, a scent that spiraled his protectiveness—already high—skyward. He shook Broderick, hand still around the wolf's throat.

Broderick wrenched himself free but kept to his feet, his Collar sparking as he came back at Ellison.

"Stop!" Maria shouted.

Broderick surprisingly obeyed, his eyes bloodshot with drink and anger. He was fairly high up in the other Shifter-town pack, the one Glory led, and he always behaved as though he had the weight of his pack behind him.

"You can't touch her until the Challenge plays out," Broderick said, rubbing his throat. "Off-limits."

"Then I'll play it out right now."

"*I* name the time and place, as the Challenged."

Ellison waited. Broderick looked Ellison up and down, keeping his sneer but with assessment in his eyes. Ellison's pack might be small, but that didn't mean Ellison had lesser power.

Maria stepped between them. Ellison sensed her panic, a primal fear that had been seared into her by the ferals who'd captured her. She was afraid of Shifters in general, but she bravely stood her ground now and held her hand out in a stopping motion to Broderick. "I can refuse the mate-claim. I know the rules."

"You're fair game, darling," Broderick said. "You need a mate to protect you."

"What I need is for both of you to leave me the hell alone!"

Broderick took a step toward her, but Ellison was around Maria with Shifter speed, blocking his path. "She refused. That's the end."

Broderick glared at Ellison, fists closing. "I'm taking this to Liam. He decides."

"He knows Shifter law."

"I know. He knows pack law too. When Andrea came here, the pack wouldn't accept her until she had a mate. We didn't need her running around making every male fight over her. The same thing applies now."

"Not with a human. She's not part of *any* pack."

"Then what's she doing here? She either follows Shifter law, or she leaves."

Maria already had left. Not being stupid, she was walking swiftly across the vacant lot, heading for the street that would lead to where she lived with Sean and Andrea, Dylan and Glory.

Ellison turned his back on Broderick and strode after her. He heard Broderick mutter something behind him, but Broderick didn't follow. Likely he was going back to the bar to either drown his troubles or whine at Liam.

Ellison quickened his footsteps to reach Maria. Broderick wasn't wrong about male Shifters wanting to fight each other over her. Females were few and far between. Unmated, unprotected females, fewer still. Most of the males were more polite than Broderick, but just barely.

Ellison, who'd watched Maria across his street every day as she'd lived, first with Liam and family, then with Sean and family, had left her alone. Having heard the story of her rescue from the feral pack by Dylan, Ellison knew Maria was still hurting.

The feral Shifters, led by a Shifter called Miguel—had kept Maria like an animal. What they'd done to her exactly, Ellison wasn't certain, and he'd never asked. She'd never talked about it, just as she'd never spoken about her time with her brother. From what Liam had said, though, her brother had treated her as though she had some contagious disease.

Maria never said a word in complaint. Ellison had watched her square her shoulders and work hard at any job she could get. She squared her shoulders now, in the white T-shirt she wore for her job at the bar, her black braid hanging down her back.

Ellison caught up to her as she walked down the middle of the quiet street. He knew Maria heard him coming—his boots clicked loudly on the asphalt—but she didn't turn to greet him.

Other Shifters were out, sitting on dark porches or running as their animals in the common yards behind the houses, or doing other things in the shadows that made him growl. Shifters were calm on their home territories, but still dangerous.

"Don't walk home alone," Ellison said harshly. He was too raw with emotion to keep his voice gentle.

"I do as I please," Maria said in a hard tone. Then her voice softened. "I'm sorry. I heard you were called home. Is Deni all right?"

"Yes." The word jerked out. Ellison was still wound up from Deni's relapse, and Broderick being an asshole hadn't helped calm him down.

"I'm really sorry." Her mouth turned down, lovely plump red lips. "Thank you for stopping Broderick."

"You refused him. Too bad. I was ready to kick his ass."

"I'm allowed to turn down mate-claims. Liam said so."

"Liam's right." Ellison moved closer to her. "But you're going to piss off every horny Shifter male by doing it. Fair warning."

"Doesn't matter. I won't live in Shiftertown forever."

Ellison didn't like that. "You can't be planning to move back in with your brother."

Maria stopped, her braid swinging. She turned warm brown eyes up to him, but they held a hint of steel. "Of course not. This is America. I don't have to live with my brother, or with Liam, or Sean. I can live in a place on my own."

"Alone?" Ellison blinked. "Why would you want to?" He couldn't imagine living by himself, without sister, nephews, cubs, parents, pack—*family*.

He was almost alone here, head of a pack of four. No mate of his own, no cubs. *Lone Wolf,* the other Shifters sometimes called him.

"It's different for me," Maria said. "The idea of being alone is ...*splendid.*"

"Lonely."

"Peaceful."

"Boring." Ellison shook his head.

"I wouldn't sit at home and do nothing. I would ..." Maria bit the corner of her lip then drew a breath. "If I tell you this, will you keep it to yourself? Andrea knows, and Glory. And Connor. No one else."

"Connor?" She named Liam's nephew, younger than Ellison's nephews, all of twenty-one.

"Yes, Connor. He's good at keeping secrets. I want to go to school. I've been saving up for it, and I'm already working on my application and looking for scholarships. Connor's been helping me study for the tests called SATs. I'll be taking them this Saturday."

"Community college? Maybe a good thing. You could drive Connor—the kid's a maniac behind the wheel."

"No, not community college. University. UT Austin."

Ellison whistled. "They don't take everyone—they don't take Shifters at all. Maybe you should start with something smaller, work your way up to it."

Her indignant look could have lit a fire. "There is no reason to start small. If you want something, you go for it. You never know in this life when it will all be taken away."

So true. Maria spoke from her own experience, and look what had happened to Deni.

Maria's anger made her shake. She needed reassurance, cried out for it, though Ellison knew she'd never admit it.

Ellison put a hand on her shoulder. Quietly, like he would for a cub who was upset.

But Maria wasn't a cub. She was a beautiful young

woman, alone, unprotected, yet gutsy and strong for what had happened to her.

Ellison's touch of reassurance turned to a caress, the backs of his fingers brushing her skin. "You go for it, Maria. Aim as high as you want." *And if you fall, I'll be here to catch you.*

Maria's expression softened. She had a round face, pretty, ringlets of black hair trickling loose from its binding. Ellison's need to kiss her rose like a newly kindled fire, to press his lips against the soft red ones, to taste the moisture inside her mouth.

"Is everything all right with Deni?" Maria asked.

"Yeah," Ellison said, jerking his gaze from her lips. "She's fine now." Ellison had left her sleeping, Andrea holding her hand.

"I'll go over and see her tomorrow, all right?"

"Yeah, she'd like that. But if she gets ... you know ... forgetful, you get out. Dominant female wolves can be very dangerous."

"She won't hurt me." Maria spoke with a confidence Ellison didn't share. Deni had been intent on killing him, her own brother.

They'd reached Sean's house, all quiet within. Ellison's house was dark as well. Maria slowed her steps and stopped with Ellison at the bottom of Sean's front porch. Silence hung between them, and warmth.

"Thank you for rescuing me," Maria said. "Twice."

Ellison reached up to tip the hat he'd left at home when he'd raced out to find her. "Any time, darlin'."

Her smile flashed, beauty in the darkness. The smile

went from polite to genuine, hot as the Texas sunshine. "*Hasta luego*," she said. *See you soon.*

Ellison made himself step away from her. The move was difficult, as though someone had wrapped elastic straps around himself and her to pull them together. "You need any more rescuing, you call me, sweetheart," he said. "Good night."

"Good night." Another flash of smile, and Maria turned, ran up onto the porch, and was gone.

Ellison stayed in the street, watching the closed door. A light went on downstairs, then off, then one upstairs, in the bedroom they'd given Maria. A glow illuminated her as she came to the window, ready to close the blind.

Maria saw Ellison, who remained staring up at her like a love-struck wolf cub. She waved then closed the blind, shutting him out.

"You plan on eating her alive?" a gravelly voice asked him.

Ellison whirled around, fist on his chest. "*Shit.* Spike."

Spike stood two feet away from Ellison, his son on his shoulders, the little boy holding on to his dad's head. Ellison hadn't heard or sensed either of them. Spike was a tracker, one of the best—good at stealth. But Ellison should have scented and sensed the cub, a four-year-old called Jordan.

"Hey, Jordan," Ellison said, trying to force himself to relax. "Taking your dad out for a walk?"

Jordan laughed. "Yeah. It's fun." Spike hadn't known about the kid until last fall, and now the two shared a bond that was like cement.

"Watch Broderick," Spike said. "He's going to try to make the mate-claim and your Challenge stick."

"Damn, word travels fast."

"Broderick went back to the bar and started pissing and moaning to Liam. Ronan got worried about Maria and called me, asking me to check on her. So here I am, checking on her. But I guess you got it covered."

He started to turn away, Spike finished.

"If the Challenge goes down, want to be my second?" Ellison asked him.

Spike called his answer over his shoulder. "Do you have to ask?" Jordan laughed and waved, and the pair of them faded into the darkness.

Ellison walked up to his front porch. From the quiet inside, everyone had gone to bed—he could hear his nephews snoring in the bedroom they shared, and the quieter breathing of Deni.

Broderick was going to be a problem. Ellison had no worries about kicking his ass, but Maria's fear had been sharp. Getting past that would be more difficult.

Ellison didn't trust Broderick not to try to climb up on Sean's porch and steal Maria out of her bedroom. Broderick would never consider doing that with a Shifter woman—not these days—but humans were regarded as weak, and Maria had already been the victim of a Shifter abduction. Broderick would figure that meant he could do what he wanted with her, and unfortunately, so might other Shifters.

Ellison sat down on one of the chairs on the porch, the chair's wood creaking. He put his feet up on the rail and leaned back, hands behind his head, to watch the square of light that was Maria's window.

The window went dark, Maria seeking her bed. She'd be

all cuddled up under the sheets, alone, not wearing much of anything. She'd smell of sweet sleep, damp skin, desire.

Ellison let out a sharp breath. If he kept his thoughts in that line, he'd be climbing up on the roof himself to steal her away. He was as bad as Broderick, and he knew it.

Ellison settled back in the chair, gaze fixed firmly on the dark window. Good thing wolves liked to stay up all night.

———

Maria opened her eyes in the dark. She smelled them around her, the women, both human and Shifter, who'd been sequestered by the ferals. With them the scents of the kids—scared, defiant, exhausted. Maria didn't need to be Shifter to understand what fear and defeat smelled like.

How own child lay in her arms. She could feel him, the weight of the little body, the warmth, the beauty of him.

But he'd been born too weak. Maria had begged Luis then Miguel to take her and him to a hospital, to a doctor at least, and Miguel wouldn't. Hours later, her son was dead

The child in her arms disappeared leaving Maria bereft, empty, grieving. She lay on the cold floor, her sobs coming, dry and broken. A hand touched her hair, the soft brush of a woman called Peigi, trying to comfort her.

There was no comfort. Maria had lost everything—family, her child, herself. She lay in the cold darkness, alone, empty. She'd never see daylight again, never feel warmth, never feel whole. She'd been broken, part of herself taken away.

In the middle of the grief came a hated voice. Peigi's

gentle touch vanished, to be replaced by a fierce grip in her hair, pulling her up.

"You're trying again," the voice said in rough Spanish. Maria had never known where Miguel had been born and raised, but he spoke several languages, fluently if not elegantly. "We need cubs that live."

Maria screamed. The scream rang through the huge basement, coming back to her in waves. The kids started to cry, the women to keen.

Miguel pulled her up, and up, and up ... and Maria was sitting in her bed in Shiftertown, her heart thudding, her breath coming in dry hiccups. She put her hand to her face and found it wet with tears.

Air, she needed air. The little room was stuffy, the nights warming now.

Maria scrambled out of bed, her legs shaking, and stumbled to the window. She cranked up the blind and opened the casement as quietly as possible.

Something moved on the porch across the street. Maria froze, ducking into the shadows of her bedroom before she worked up the courage to peer out again.

She saw a pair of cowboy boots propped up on the porch railing, and long legs going back into shadow. Maria's body relaxed, her racing heart slowing.

She crept across the room to her dresser and found the pair of binoculars Sean had given her when she'd expressed interest in bird-watching down at the river. Right now she wanted to do a little Shifter-watching.

Maria returned to the window and trained the binoculars onto Ellison Rowe's porch. There he was, leaning back in a wooden porch chair, eyes closed, mouth slightly open.

She couldn't hear from here, but she knew soft snores issued from his mouth.

Maria smiled, the fear of the dream vanishing. The grief didn't lessen, and it would never go away, but her emptiness receded a little. The cowboy across the street, who'd come to her rescue twice tonight, was here with her. She wasn't alone.

———

Ellison went inside in the morning, stiff, groggy, and having no idea how he'd fallen asleep in the chair.

All looked normal at Sean's, and at Liam's house next door to it. Kim had tripped off to work, Andrea's boy was wailing with his usual energy, and Connor came out to work on Dylan's truck, along with Tiger, another rescue from captivity.

Tiger glanced over at Ellison but didn't return Ellison's wave of greeting. Not that Ellison expected a Shifter who'd spent his entire life in a cage to know how to respond, or to care.

Tiger hauled up the truck's hood and bent over it, starting to tinker, with Connor's help. Working on vehicles seemed to be the only thing that kept Tiger calm.

Ellison showered, shaved, and came out of his room to see Deni cooking breakfast with Will. Jackson had already left for a job he had with a moving company. Will worked at a furniture warehouse. Shifters were good at lifting and carrying.

Deni looked rested, cheerful even. Ellison put his arm

around her as she stirred the mess of eggs and cubed potatoes in the frying pan and kissed her cheek.

"Don't put too much salt in mine," he said.

"Don't backseat cook." Deni smiled at him, and Ellison's heart lightened.

It would lighten even more when he saw Maria. Ellison told Deni he'd be right back, gave Will a brief hug, caught up his hat, and walked out the door.

Running across the street to see how Maria was doing after she'd been badgered last night would be the neighborly thing to do. Right? Ellison could pretend he'd come to get a taste of whatever pancakes Sean was cooking today.

Andrea met him at the door, with little Kenny Morrissey, her firstborn, on her hip.

"Maria? No, she's not here," Andrea said. "She left without a word very early this morning, and I don't know where she is. I was hoping she was with you and Den."

CHAPTER FOUR

Maria. Missing. And Andrea stood there calmly, cuddling her son, like nothing was wrong.

"What do you mean, you don't know where she is?"

Ellison took a broad step forward, his wolf growling all the way.

A mistake—a big mistake. Sean materialized out of the kitchen, holding a pancake turner. His eyes were Shifter white, focused on Ellison, the lion in him responding to a threat to his mate, his cub, his territory.

The Guardian was the last person a Shifter would ever see, the point of the Guardian's sword sending the Shifter's soul to the afterlife. Whatever else Sean might be—friend, mate, tracker—he was also death.

Ellison stepped back, hands up, trying to show Sean that he meant no harm—to Sean's house, mate, cub, or pancakes.

"Why don't you know where she is?" Ellison asked Andrea.

"She was gone when we woke up," Andrea said. "Or at

least when I checked on her. I was up early, with Kenny, and I heard the back door close."

Which explained why Ellison hadn't seen Maria go. Or else she'd left while Ellison had been in the shower. *Shit.*

"Did you call her?" Ellison demanded.

"Of course I did," Andrea said. "No answer. Left a voice mail."

Ellison didn't need to ask Andrea for Maria's number. He'd memorized it a while back. "And you don't have any idea where she went?"

Sean stepped in front of Andrea, though the deadly look had faded from his eyes. "Come in and have pancakes, Ellison. I'll make some with pecans. Your favorite."

They were trying to placate him. *Calm the wolf down.*

Kenny was looking at Ellison with round gray eyes, his mouth working on one fist. Shifters of crossed species were born in human form and revealed their Shifter form when they were about two or three. Sean was Feline, Andrea Lupine—Kenny could go either way. From his eyes though, Ellison would bet wolf.

"Thanks, but I'll pass," Ellison said. "Where was Maria planning to go? She say anything to you last night?"

"We don't keep her prisoner," Andrea returned, irritated. "She comes and goes when she wants, wherever she wants. She doesn't have to check with us."

The reasonable part of Ellison knew Andrea was right, but the Shifter part of him didn't give a crap.

"She needs to check in when Shifters are threatening to start their own personal breeding projects with her. Tell you what—she can come and live in my house. I'll look out for her better."

Sean's expression hardened. "Not gonna happen."

Liam's stipulation when Maria had come to Shiftertown was that, while she could take a room with whomever she chose, she couldn't live in the house of an unmated male, for obvious reasons. She'd lived for a time in Liam's house with Connor there, because he hadn't made his Transition yet, and the mating need hadn't yet manifested in him.

But once Tiger had moved in last November, Maria had to vacate. She'd moved in with Andrea and Sean, Dylan and Glory without fuss, understanding, she said.

That Andrea didn't know where she'd gone bothered Ellison a lot.

"She needs looking after," Ellison growled. "If y'all can't do it, we need to find someone who can."

He swung around and walked off the porch, not slowing down. "Where are you going?" Andrea called worriedly behind him.

"To look for her. Where'd you think?"

The scenario in his head went like this—Maria gets up early, deciding to find Connor and study for her SATs with him. She walks out the back door, and Broderick is lying in wait. Ellison is in the shower, and Broderick drags her off.

Anything human in Ellison disappeared. He'd already claimed Maria, in his head and in his heart. He'd held off, because Dylan had explained exactly what had happened to her down in Mexico. *Give her time,* Dylan had said. *Liam, Sean, and I will protect her until she's ready.*

Ellison was ready. He'd kill Broderick and bounce his head down the sidewalk if the Lupine had touched Maria. Ellison's Collar sparked with his adrenaline, warning him to calm down, but Ellison told his Collar to take a flying leap.

Broderick lived two blocks over and two blocks down. A short distance for wolves who were used to patrolling vast tracts of territory.

Ellison approached the two-story bungalow that housed Broderick, his mother, aunt, and three brothers. Youngest brother was on the porch shoveling food from a plate into his mouth but was on his feet by the time Ellison reached the front steps.

"Stay right there, wolf," the brother, Mason, said.

"Get Broderick out here so I can rip his head off."

Mason set down his plate of eggs and toast and stood up squarely. He was the youngest brother, but he was bigger than any of the others in Broderick's house, probably why they had him stand guard.

"Brod!" Mason yelled over his shoulder. "That dumb-ass Lupine is here."

"I heard him." Broderick came out the door to flank his brother. He folded his arms, the pair of them glaring down at Ellison with identical stares. "What? It's early. Why aren't you holed up with your crazy sister?"

"Where is she?"

Broderick didn't move. "You mean Maria? Not here. Why?"

Ellison leaned toward Broderick and inhaled, too far gone in rage to care that it wasn't good Shifter etiquette to obviously check someone's scent to determine whether he was lying. Especially not on that rival Shifter's territory with his little brother ready to rub Ellison's face into the sidewalk.

Ellison didn't smell a lie on Broderick, but he didn't smell Maria on him either. He caught the brief scent of her from last night, when Broderick had tried to mark her and claim her, but nothing more than that. Scents had layers, fading with time and how many showers the Shifter had taken. Broderick hadn't bathed since last night, but his clothes were clean and contained no scent of Maria.

"What did you do, lose her?" Broderick asked. "Doesn't she live across the street from you?"

"Screw you." Maria wasn't here. If she had been, even if they'd locked her in the most protected part of their basement, Ellison would have scented her and found her.

Ellison spun away from the porch and started down the street again, worry piling on worry. The sky was blue, the sun bright, another beautiful day in Austin. The sunlight would sparkle in Maria's dark hair, dance on her smile.

Footsteps sounded beside him, and then Ellison got a full dose of Broderick's unwashed scent. "So where is she?"

"Would I be here ready to kill you if I knew?"

Broderick didn't answer, but he didn't leave either. "I'm coming with you," he said.

"The fuck you are."

"You aren't doing a very good job of finding her, are you? Two heads better than one."

"But I want your head on the ground," Ellison growled.

"That's where I want yours. But we find Maria first. Sure she's not with one of the Morrisseys?"

"No. And they don't seem worried."

"Fucked-up Feline bastards."

Ellison ignored Broderick the best he could as he made his way back to Liam's house. Connor and Tiger were still bent over Dylan's truck.

Ellison stopped outside the property line and hauled Broderick back before the man could run up to Connor, likely to close his hand around Connor's neck and demand the cub to tell what he knew.

If Broderick did that, he'd lose his arm, because Tiger was already straightening up from behind the hood and glaring at them with those weird eyes of his. Tiger, though only adopted into Liam's family and clan, was seriously protective of Connor.

Tiger hadn't been born of Shifter parents—he'd been bred in a research facility and raised in a cage by human scientists for about forty years. They'd been trying to create a super-Shifter—one who was better, stronger, faster, and all that shit, than your average Shifter. They were trying to do what the Fae had done a couple thousand years ago, except without the magic and possibly not the maniacal laughter. The single-minded cruelty had been there, though.

The result was Tiger—superstrong, barely controlled, and not happy with people who messed with Connor. He wore a Collar, but Ellison was one of the few who knew the Collar was fake. Liam had tried to put a real one on Tiger and it hadn't worked, so a fake one had to do for now.

The man didn't have a name, either. Tiger didn't know what it was—the humans who'd created him had called him Twenty-Three. The woman who'd rescued him had decreed that Tiger could pick his own name, but so far, he hadn't. So everyone called him Tiger.

Tiger wasn't growling, but he didn't need to. The stare from the yellow eyes was enough.

"Connor," Ellison said.

"Yep?" Connor answered, wiping his hands.

"You take Maria somewhere this morning?"

"Nope. But if you're asking if I've seen her, I did. She

came out the back door bright and early, said hi to me, said she was going to help Ronan look after Olaf, and said to tell you she could hear you snoring all the way across the street."

Broderick made a sound that was a cross between a snort and a laugh. Tiger said nothing at all.

"Damn it." Common sense told Ellison he was running around Shiftertown making an idiot of himself, but his hackles still wouldn't go down. Something was wrong—didn't matter if he didn't know what. Didn't matter that everyone else was being logical and unworried.

"Thanks, Connor," he managed to say. "If she comes back, tell her to stay put, will you?"

"Sure thing."

Tiger's gaze remained fixed, the big man with his mixed black and orange hair focused in silence on Ellison.

"We go to Ronan's then?" Broderick asked.

"*I'll* go to Ronan's. You go home."

"Like I'm letting a Lupine from another pack tell me what to do. I don't like wolves from my *own* pack telling me what to do."

Annoying asshole. Ellison tried to ignore him as he plotted a course for Ronan's, and started between the houses to get to the common.

"I will come with you."

Tiger stepped into their path before Ellison saw the guy move. He was about three inches taller than Ellison, as big as a bear Shifter. He'd be great to have on hand if Ellison needed help with a fight. On the other hand, Tiger was unpredictable, stronger than any Shifter he knew, and not quite stable in the head.

"You need to take care of Connor," Ellison said.

Tiger remained in place, a wall Ellison wasn't going to get around. "I will come with you."

"It's all right," Connor said, more to Tiger than Ellison. "I'll be fine."

Tiger nodded once and turned away, starting off in the direction of Ronan's.

Connor stepped to Ellison and spoke in a low voice. "Keep an eye on him. Tiger, I mean. He's usually fine, but when he gets upset ..."

"Yeah, I know what he does. I'm having a great morning—my girl's missing, and now I'm babysitting a crazy Shifter and a wolf from a rival pack."

"Tiger's not crazy," Connor said. "Just ... intense."

"Intense. Right."

The way Tiger turned around and stared back at them told Ellison he'd heard every word.

"Don't worry, I'll take care of him." Ellison growled again, ruffled Connor's hair, and walked rapidly after Tiger and Broderick.

———

One of the foster kids at Ronan's—Cherie—told them that Maria had come for Olaf early and the two had gone off together. Cherie was a cub going on twenty-one, with brown and lighter brown hair that marked her as a grizzly. She was yawning, the only one at Ronan's house, and barely awake. Ronan had asked Maria to look after Olaf today, Cherie explained, while everyone else was out. Maria had seemed happy to.

Cherie looked annoyed to be roused out of her sleep-in, but bears were like that. They loved their sleep.

"Where did she take him?" Ellison asked.

"Walking." She shrugged. "I don't know. Maria's trust-worthy, and Olaf likes her. They'll be fine." Cherie looked over the three male Shifters as though they didn't impress her, named a park outside Shiftertown where Olaf liked to go, and retreated with a decisive bang of the door.

The park wasn't far, a good brisk walk out the other side of Shiftertown and down a few streets. The roads were quiet here, with little traffic. No drivers to stare at Ellison, Broder-ick, and the giant Tiger with his orange and black hair bringing up the rear.

The park lay vast, green, and open, the eastern edge of it running up to a little ridge full of dense trees. A few joggers shuffled around the paths, but kids had already gone to school, and most adults to work. One or two moms pushed kids in strollers, but the park was largely empty.

No sign of Maria's dark hair and lovely body, no woman tugging a ten-year-old boy with white hair with her along the paths.

Ellison made for the ridge on the other side. Something pulled him that way, a sense of wrongness. He walked faster and faster, running by the time he took a path that led over a stream, up some stone steps, into the woods that led up the side of the hill.

Tiger heard her first. He grabbed Ellison by the shoulder and silently pointed a broad finger into deeper shadows, where the hill climbed high.

Ellison let Tiger, with his better hearing and sight, lead. Tiger moved noiselessly, fading into the woods like smoke. If

Ellison hadn't kept a sharp eye on him, he'd have quickly lost him.

"Olaf!" Maria's voice came to them before they'd walked another twenty yards. "*Olaf!*"

The word had an echoing quality, as though she'd gone into a cavern or tunnel. Ellison jogged to catch up with Tiger, who quietly led him down another little hill into a tiny valley.

The valley ran between the ridge and another hill on the other side. On top of the second hill was a road shielded by a concrete barrier. Cars raced along it, the drivers paying no attention to what was below them.

A wide culvert opened under the road. Maria stood a few feet inside it, hands around her mouth, calling desperately for Olaf.

CHAPTER FIVE

Maria peered into the darkness, straining to see Olaf. She'd taken two steps into the chilly culvert into which he'd disappeared before she'd frozen, unable to move.

The press of the concrete walls, the cold dampness, the dank smell, very like that in the basement of the warehouse in which she'd been kept, triggered memories too powerful to stop. Her heart constricted, her throat working while she fought down the screams.

Only Olaf's little growls—telling her he'd shifted into his polar bear cub—kept her from running out, back into the sunshine, back to Shiftertown.

"Olaf, please come back." Her voice was shaking, but she knew her pleas would have little impact. Olaf would have decided by now that Maria wouldn't come in there after him.

She heard footsteps behind her, heavy ones, made by the firm strides of Shifters.

In her state, Maria's mind told her they were Miguel's

Shifters, come to find her. She clamped her mouth closed over her cries of panic and fled into the tunnel.

"Maria!"

The sound of the warm voice made Maria stop, her breath hurting her.

Ellison. An anchor, shelter from the cold. Maria turned back, something heating in her when she saw his tall silhouette at the tunnel's opening, his big cowboy hat a comforting sight.

She took a few running steps toward Ellison, then stopped again as two other Shifters appeared behind him. One was Broderick—what was *he* doing here? The other was the Tiger-man who lived in Liam's house. Maria wasn't afraid of him exactly—Tiger had never paid her much attention—but his bulk was frightening in the darkness of the culvert.

Ellison didn't wait. He came into the tunnel, his long legs bringing him to her in a few strides. "Maria, honey, you all right?"

He slid his arm around her waist. He did it without thought, the most natural thing in the world.

Maria managed a nod. "It's Olaf. He's gone exploring and won't come out."

Ellison was like a rock. His arm steadied her, and his warmth at her side quieted her fears. His hat touched her hair, and then she felt his lips on the top of her head.

"Stay put," he said. "I'll get him. Tiger—look after Maria."

"I'll watch her," Broderick said, too quickly.

"No. You'll come with me."

"Chase bears yourself, Rowe," Broderick said with a growl. "I'll take Maria home."

His arrogance snapped something inside Maria. The fiery temper she'd been ashamed of before her abduction reared up. "You get in there and find Olaf," she said to Broderick, pointing her finger down the tunnel. "If he doesn't come out, or one hair on his pelt is hurt, you can explain to Ronan why you didn't go in after him."

Ellison chuckled, more heat. "I know who my money's on."

Broderick growled again. "You're going to leave her with the crazy?"

Tiger said absolutely nothing, but when his yellow eyes flicked to Broderick, Broderick swallowed.

Maria took a step closer to Tiger. "I'll be fine. Get Olaf."

Broderick made another snarling noise but took off down the tunnel.

"Be right back," Ellison said. He touched his hat brim, gave Maria his big smile, and jogged down the tunnel after Broderick.

———

THE WOLF IN ELLISON DIDN'T LIKE THE TUNNEL OF THE culvert. Wolves preferred wide meadows, where they could run, or the quiet of woods that flowed for miles. Wild wolves did hole up in dens, but those were shallow caves, not deep tunnels.

The dislike of caves came from racial memory, maybe. The Fae had liked caves, not to live in, but as a place in which to keep their slaves. Slaves meant Shifters. That is, until the Shifters had told the Fae to go fuck themselves and had fought a long, bloody war for their freedom.

Ellison's Lupine Shifter ancestors had been thrilled to be free of the underground, to run in the wild, where they belonged.

Bears, on the other hand …

"Why does he want to explore down here?" Broderick asked, a shudder in his voice.

"Bears. Damn things *like* caves."

"But he's a polar bear."

"So maybe he likes ice caves."

"Let's find the shit and get him out of here," Broderick said. "It'll make the woman happy."

The woman. That was how he talked about Maria, the beautiful lady Broderick said he wanted to mate-claim. Dickhead.

Ellison had drunk in the beauty of her, even as he'd worried for Olaf. She wore form-hugging jeans today and a tight-fitting shirt, a black elbow-sleeved T with spangled red and blue flowers on the front, two small buttons holding it closed at the very top. She was a delicious package. Ellison wanted to find Olaf quickly so he could return and enjoy it.

"Olaf!" Ellison called, his voice falling against the dead air of the tunnel. "Where are you?"

If they lost Olaf, it wasn't only Maria he'd have to face. Ronan loved the kid. Olaf was an orphan of unknown clan who'd needed a home, and Ronan had volunteered his. Ronan was always doing things like that, the big, giant softie.

The big, giant softie had foot-long claws, and teeth that could rip a tree in half.

A trickle of water sounded up ahead, the tunnel built to

carry runoff from creeks when they overflowed. Ellison always found it fascinating that Austin was crisscrossed by creeks and wetlands, while other parts of the vast state, not very far from here even, were bone-dry. Texas and its amazing diversity went on forever.

Ellison heard Olaf growl. A long, low growl, from a baby animal throat, at something that had the cub surprised and worried. Olaf was a fairly fearless little guy, so anything that worried him worried Ellison.

Ellison stripped off his boots, ready to let his wolf come out.

Shifting wasn't always instantaneous. Ellison's body fought it today, both human and wolf wanting to hurry and find Olaf and take him out. He willed himself to be wolf—easier to track, easier to fight in that form.

He shucked his jeans as his legs started to bend to the wolf's, fur swiftly erasing his human flesh. Once Ellison's four wolf feet hit the ground, the struggle ceased, and the wolf took over.

He pinpointed Broderick's rank smell right away and ran past it, Broderick a smudge in the darkness. Up ahead, Olaf was still growling, throwing off agitated bear cub smell.

Ellison also scented Tiger and Maria behind him. Tiger was the musky male at the top of his strength. Maria was the gentler of the two, like the cinnamon and honey she put on her buñuelos. She smelled of home and things of light, a beacon in the darkness.

Ellison knew she'd hesitated following Olaf because the underground reminded her too much of her captivity. Ellison and she shared that hatred of the close darkness, which represented to both of them imprisonment, slavery, and terror.

Another odor assaulted Ellison's nose and had Broderick growling. Humans. Human men not as afraid of confronting a polar bear Shifter as they should be.

They weren't afraid *yet*. Ellison sped up and charged around a corner into a second culvert.

Three human men stood inside the tunnel, blocking the way to daylight behind them. LED lanterns threw pale shadows on the ceiling and over the polar bear cub who stood defiantly before them. One man had a tranquilizer rifle, pointed at Olaf, and the other two held a large net between them.

Ellison took this in with rapid calculation before he gave in to his wolf's rage. He charged, his Collar sparking hard.

The scent from the men changed to panic. Facing a full-grown Shifter wolf was a different thing from facing a bear cub, though they'd have found Olaf a handful. But the gunman still had the tranq rifle, and he raised it to point it at Ellison.

Ellison let his body hit the ground, under the rifle's aim. He slammed himself at the gunman, sweeping him from his feet. The man yelped as Ellison ran into him, and dropped the rifle, which went off as it spun around, the tranq dart flying. The dart hit nothing, clattering to the floor to be lost in the darkness.

In the next moment, Broderick came running in, in the form of his timber wolf. He hurtled toward the men with the net, his Collar snapping sparks, but Broderick didn't let the Collar slow him down. The net men spun with quick reflexes, ready to snare him.

They'd done this before, Ellison realized. The three men worked as a well-practiced team, the rifleman rolling to pick up the rifle and reload it while the men with the net regrouped. In a second, they'd have the thing over Broderick.

Ellison went for the gunman again. His heavy wolf body crushed the man into the nearest wall, making him drop the rifle once more, and Ellison heard a bone snap.

Sparks zapped Ellison hard, and pain ran like fire through every nerve. Fucking Collar. Ellison could control the Collar when he fought in the rings at the Shifter fight club, because his brain knew then that he didn't really want to kill the Shifter against him.

But these humans had threatened a *cub*, and Ellison wanted them dead. The Collar sensed his need to kill and went to work trying to stop him. The Collars evened the odds, in spite of the gunman's broken wrist, and the net that had started to tangle Broderick.

Olaf ran back and forth between the men, growling up a storm, grabbing legs and heels, biting.

"Shoot him!" One of the net men yelled. "Grab that damned bear, and let's get out of here."

"He broke my arm!" the gunman shouted back.

"Sixteen million! Think about sixteen million."

Sixteen million dollars? Did they mean for Olaf?

Screw the Collar. Ellison slammed his body into the human's again, letting his Collar's sparks strike the man's flesh. The man screamed, another bone or two definitely breaking.

Broderick fought and writhed, but the net, which appeared to be barbed in places, had closed around him. One of the men dropped his end of the net and dove for the rifle, coming up with it and the dart full of tranquilizer before Ellison could stop him.

And then the tunnel filled with noise, a roaring sound with death in it. The man who'd grabbed the gun executed a practiced roll, got to his feet, and shot the tranquilizer dart straight at the giant tiger that hurtled in from the darkness end of the tunnel.

The tiger was so big that he broke off pieces off the wall as he charged. The dart hit Tiger in the chest...

... and didn't slow him a step. The rage in Tiger's eyes escalated to madness as he kept on coming.

The man trying to contain Broderick dropped the net and fled. The first gunman squirmed out from behind Ellison and ran up the tunnel toward daylight, staggering and cradling his broken arm.

The man who'd shot the tranq at Tiger stood frozen in stark terror. Tiger was going to kill him.

Tiger had killed once before, Ellison knew, though the Shifters were keeping it quiet. Not Tiger's fault, Liam had said. Human scientists had created Tiger to be a killing machine, and Tiger didn't yet know how not to be.

But if Tiger was arrested for killing a human, Shifter Bureau might find out who Tiger was and what he was, and take him away. Back to a lab, or maybe they'd just outright slaughter him. And Liam and the rest of Shiftertown would pay for harboring him.

Ellison morphed back to his human self, landing panting, upright on his feet. "Run, you idiot," he said to the remaining man. "I can't stop him."

The human remained rooted in place, staring in horrified wonder as Tiger unfolded from the giant Bengal and became a giant human, his eyes still yellow with fury. The dart stuck out of Tiger's muscled chest, and Tiger contemptuously yanked it out.

"Leave. The cub. Alone." The words were guttural, harsh, inhuman.

The man blinked, gulped a breath, and finally turned to flee. Ellison grabbed the tranq rifle out of the man's hands as he ran by. Ellison raced after him but stopped inside the shadows of the culvert while the man sprinted after his friends into the bright light of morning.

Ellison watched him scramble into a waiting high-end SUV, a cage obvious in the back. The vehicle squealed away, leaving the faint bite of exhaust in the warm spring breeze.

Tiger ran a few steps past Ellison and stopped, not bothering to keep his large, naked body out of the sunlight. "You let them go." He turned back and bent his angry gaze on Ellison. "They were going to hurt the cub."

"No, they were going to *steal* the cub," Ellison said. He leaned against the cool tunnel wall to catch his breath. "I don't know what that's about."

"I would have killed them first."

"I know." Ellison gathered his courage and reached to place his hand on Tiger's formidable bicep. "If you'd killed any of them, hell would rain down on Shifters, and you'd be captured, and possibly killed and dissected. Connor's trusting me to keep you out of trouble, remember?"

Tiger jerked away from Ellison's touch. "They can't hurt the cubs."

Tiger was ferociously protective of all cubs—he'd lost the only one of his own, the humans wrenching it away from him before he could properly know it or say good-bye. Liam speculated that he transferred that grief into being crazily protective of the cubs in Shiftertown.

Ellison shared that obsessive protectiveness—most Shifters had it—but Tiger took it over the top.

"Trust me, big guy, there are other ways," Ellison said. "We have their equipment, and I got a good look at them and their SUV. We'll find them and persuade them it's a bad idea to mess with us. Kidnapping Shifters is against human law too, and Kim knows cops who are sympathetic to Shifters. We'll get them."

Tiger looked unconvinced. But at least he turned away and went back into the tunnel.

Broderick was just finishing fighting his way out of the net. "Bastards, fucking bastards. Why didn't you kill them?"

Ellison didn't bother explaining a second time. "Where's Maria?"

Olaf, still a bear, was dancing around, growling and beating the air, doing a little victory hop as though he'd chased off the bad guys single-handedly. The joys of being a cub.

"Maria is safe," Tiger said.

As soon as the words left his mouth, Maria's voice came up the tunnel. "Olaf? Is Olaf all right? What is happening?"

Maria followed her voice, her words dying as she ran into the light of the LED lanterns and found herself facing three large, naked Shifters and one cavorting polar bear cub.

Ellison watched her expression turn from concern for Olaf to shock at the three tall Shifters with animal rage in their eyes, and then dissolve to stark, remembered terror. He'd seen the same look on Deni's face last night when she hadn't recognized Ellison, her own brother. Maria was reliving a moment of her captivity.

She shook it off in the next second, grabbed Olaf by the scruff, and started dragging him back down the tunnel the way she'd come. The little bear dug in his feet in and wailed in protest, but Maria was relentless.

The heightened senses of Ellison's wolf felt her grief and fear, her fight for sanity. He wanted to find the Shifters who'd hurt Maria and grind them to powder.

He motioned for the other two to stay back, and ran down the tunnel after her.

CHAPTER SIX

Maria didn't stop when she heard Ellison calling her name. She continued walking swiftly, pulling Olaf with her. The bear still protested, but he'd quit fighting her, seeming to understand that she'd won.

Maria didn't halt until she reached the sunlight and the spot where she'd dropped her big shoulder bag to go running inside after Olaf. She leaned against the stone wall outside the culvert, absorbing the warmth of the concrete, and closed her eyes.

Her heart still raced in panic, her breath choking her. She knew, logically, that the Shifters inside the tunnels were her friends—except maybe Broderick—not the evil beasts who'd imprisoned her.

Even Broderick followed Shifter rules whether he liked them or not. He and the other Austin Shifters understood that they had to curb their feral tendencies in order to survive. Miguel and his pack hadn't.

"Maria."

Ellison was there, in front of her. He'd resumed his jeans, but he held his shirt crumpled in one hand.

In spite of her shakes, Maria couldn't help reflecting that Ellison was breathtaking. His jeans rode low on his hips, his liquid, tanned skin smooth over a hard body. A few red abrasions decorated his chest, and he had a solid bruise on his cheek. The worst wound was around his neck, where the Collar had burned his skin.

Her visions of the feral Shifters dissolved as concern replaced fear.

"Are you all right?" Maria reached up and touched his Collar. The black and silver entwined metal was cool under her fingertips, but she knew it had been hot and painful a few moments ago.

Ellison's gray eyes went quiet under her touch, his gaze fixing sharply on her. "Yeah, I'm OK. What about you?"

Ellison always mitigated his wolf stare for Maria, but even so, it was hard to take. Maria abruptly pulled her hand away. "I need to go home."

After a few more beats of stare, Ellison picked up the bag she'd left on the ground.

"Come on then." He put his hand on her shoulder and steered her toward the path that would lead them back to the park. "Tiger's going to sit on Broderick a while, so you don't need to worry about him."

"I'm not." Maria couldn't explain what she felt, words leaving her, so she just walked.

Having Ellison next to her, warm and tall, comforted her beyond what she could think. His hand on her shoulder held strength, but gentled for her as usual, to reassure rather than frighten.

When Maria had rushed into the culvert, worry for Olaf overriding her fears, Ellison had just finished shifting. His naked body had been beautiful, with the fire of the wolf still in his eyes. Now he was Ellison again, soothing her, helping her.

Olaf, as a bear cub, scampered ahead of them then ran back, circling their legs, enjoying himself. His clothes and things were in Maria's bag, but Olaf showed no sign of wanting to change back to a human boy.

They walked back across the ridge and down to the park, Ellison's hand steadying her. A few humans they passed did a double-take at the polar bear cub romping after butterflies, though most people who used this park knew that it lay close to Shiftertown and had grown used to Maria walking with cubs out here.

Ellison was silent as they wound through the park and walked down the few blocks to Shiftertown. Olaf ran ahead of them through the open gates. He spied another cub in a yard down the street and charged to him, the little wolf rising to meet him.

Maria started a few steps after Olaf, but a Shifter woman came out onto her porch, laughing at the two cubs, and calling a greeting to Olaf. Everyone knew Olaf, and everyone liked him. Olaf and the wolf started a mock wrestling match, Olaf none the worse for his ordeal.

Ellison pulled Maria to a halt in the shade of a tall live oak, the tree screening them from most of the houses. His fingers were warm on her shoulder, but firm. He wanted her to stay there.

"You had a flashback in that culvert, didn't you?" Ellison watched her, knowing the truth, but willing her to tell him.

Maria evaded his gaze. "I don't want to talk about it."

"I think you need to talk about it a little." Ellison touched her chin. "You know you don't need to be afraid anymore, Maria. No one will hurt you, or make you do anything you don't want to. And not just because the Morrisseys say so. *I* won't let anyone hurt you. I'll break all their fingers if they even try."

He meant it. She'd seen how he'd been with Broderick last night, ready to kill the other wolf.

Maria never knew what to say to Ellison when he was being gentle and helpful. The only thing she could think of was, "You are all so kind to me."

"Hey, it's not *kindness,* sweetheart. At least not from me." Ellison's touch went to her cheek, the caress light.

Warmth spread down through her chest. Maria tried to speak, to explain, but her lips couldn't form the words. She still struggled to think in English, and Ellison didn't know much Spanish.

"You're here, Maria. Safe." Ellison traced her cheek, increasing the warmth. "Not in the dark anymore. You don't need to be afraid. And if you are afraid, you come to me."

Maria managed a smile. "And you'll make it all better?"

"I want to."

He leaned closer, and Maria's back met the bole of the big tree. Ellison smelled of sweat and a small bite of blood, and of himself. The feral Shifters—all of them—had always stank. Ellison smelled of warmth and goodness.

Maria turned her face up to him, rising on tiptoe to offer the kiss she wanted to give him. She couldn't think of words, but she could show him with this.

She found herself caught hard against Ellison's bare

chest, his hand snaking under her braid, he leaning into her. His mouth fit clumsily to hers, his lips moving before Maria was ready. Their teeth bumped, and Ellison lifted away, laughing a little, his eyes full of heat.

"Shifters don't kiss much," he said. "At least, I don't."

There hadn't been much kissing in the feral pack either. No tenderness, not even between the males and females who'd cared for each other.

"Nuzzling, yes." Ellison leaned to her again, his nose touching her cheek, his breath warm. "I guess when you have a lot of nose, you tend to use it."

Maria wanted to laugh. No, not to laugh. To go quiet while he nuzzled her cheekbone.

"I never kissed much either," she said. When Luis had wooed her in the moonlight, before she'd known he was a Shifter, she hadn't kissed him.

This was new to her, as was Ellison's gentleness. Luis had charmed her with his dangerousness, exciting to a naive and sheltered young woman like Maria. Ellison mitigated his strength for her, showing her he'd never let loose and hurt her.

"We can learn together," Ellison said, breath against her lips.

Maria formed an unpracticed pucker, her blood warming as Ellison responded with light pressure. His hand, shirt still dangling from it, went to the tree, his lips firming against her mouth.

Maria felt the strength of his entire body through the kiss, like a hum in the air between them, as Ellison licked softly across her lips. She tasted salt and coffee on him, and a bite of himself.

She clenched her hands at her sides. She could barely breathe, nothing existing but Ellison's lips connecting with hers, his mouth tenderly prying hers open, his fingers working under her braid, loosening it.

Another kiss, another slide of his tongue between her lips. Maria flicked her tongue over his in answer, the velvet heat of it stealing her breath.

She should be afraid. She'd been afraid for such a long time. Ellison stood over her, his body against hers, pinning her with his mouth, his presence, himself. Maria should be afraid and want to duck away from him, to run, but she stayed, letting her hand steal to his chest.

She warmed as she contacted the smooth heat of his bare skin, the wiry curls that dusted his chest. She found his heartbeat, his heart drumming as rapidly as hers.

Maria slid her hand up to his neck, feeling the Collar around his throat, the raw skin it had burned. He'd been hurt, while he'd fought for Olaf, but he hadn't stopped until Olaf was safe. She didn't understand the whole story of what had happened inside the culvert, but she was too full of Ellison's taste and warmth to break away and ask.

He laced his fingers through her hair, caressing her neck as he deepened the kiss. Heat, sunlight, everything that was good and warm—Ellison.

Ellison slid his hand down her neck to her back, the other still supporting him against the tree, the softness of his dangling shirt brushing her shoulder. Maria leaned into his embrace, the sweetness of his kiss unknotting her stomach. She flowed into comfort, into wanting.

A small growl sounded, then air whooshed by her.

Ellison broke the kiss, his legs bending as the whirlwind of Olaf smacked the backs of his knees.

"Hey." Ellison turned around, his big hand still steady against Maria. He'd never let her fall.

Olaf shook himself like a dog and rose up into the form of a small boy with white hair and dark eyes. "I'm hungry!"

Maria sucked in a breath, the taste of Ellison lingering and heady. "You already had breakfast, Olaf."

"But I want pancakes. Can we go see Sean? Where's Tiger?"

Olaf rarely spoke much—the poor kid had watched his parents be shot to death. To have three or four sentences in a row come out of his mouth was unusual.

"Tiger's walking Broderick home," Ellison said. He straightened up from the tree, but he didn't take his arm from around Maria. "We'll walk with Maria to Sean's house and hit him up for pancakes. All right?"

"Yay!" Olaf grabbed Maria's hand. "Were those men trying to kidnap me, Uncle Ellison?"

"Kidnap?" Maria's eyes widened, some of the warmth evaporating. "What happened?"

"Some men tried to grab me. I smacked them." Olaf danced back, swatting with his hands as he would his bear paws.

Ellison looked grim. "Guys in an expensive SUV," he said. "Their tranq gun was top of the line too."

Olaf had opened Maria's bag and was pulling out his clothes. "Why were they trying to kidnap *me*?"

"I have some ideas," Ellison said.

Maria bent down to help Olaf pull his shirt over his head. "We need to get him home."

"But Ellison chased them off," Olaf said, his rumpled head appearing through the shirt's neckband. "He fought them with his wolf." He growled again and punched the air, his shirtsleeves flailing. "And then Tiger came. It was awesome."

Maria grabbed Olaf's hands and thrust them inside the sleeves. "Home. *Now.*"

She tried to berate herself for stopping to kiss Ellison instead of taking Olaf to safety, but the imprint of Ellison's lips remained on hers. The kiss had opened something inside her, as did the smile Ellison sent her now as he caught Olaf's other hand.

What had started to open Maria never wanted to close again.

———

"You got the license number, then?" Dylan Morrissey, who showed his nearly three hundred years of age only by the gray-flecked hair at his temples, gave Ellison his powerful alpha stare.

Dylan was no longer leader of Shiftertown, but he was still one of the strongest Shifters around.

As Lupine, Ellison should go into intense defensive mode under Dylan's questioning, but because the Morrisseys had accepted Ellison as friend long ago, and because Ellison worked for Liam as a tracker—bodyguard, investigator, enforcer—Dylan was going easy on him. Ellison pushed his instincts aside and answered.

"License plate number, make of the car, description of the guys. It's all in here." Ellison tapped his head. "Tiger saw them too, but he was in killer mode, so who knows what he remembers."

"Tiger and Ellison kicked butt," Olaf said.

Olaf remained at Dylan and Sean's house. Maria, once she'd heard the full story, insisted that the cub shouldn't go home until Ronan could be there to take care of him. Ronan, alerted by Ellison, was on his way, and he agreed Olaf should stay at Dylan's, one of the safest houses in Shiftertown, until he arrived.

Maria played with snap-together blocks with Olaf, the kid building some kind of robot monster with it. From a movie, but Ellison didn't know which one. The only movies Ellison watched were Westerns. The remake of *3:10 to Yuma* was his current favorite, even though it wasn't set in Texas.

Maria's black braid was mussed from Ellison working his fingers through it. He could still feel the amazing heavy silk of her hair, that and the taste of her. Honey, sweetness, fire. Maria.

She was resilient, protective, defiant, and soft all at the same time. Like a rose—fragile but tough.

Maria helped Olaf build the robot with confident hands. She'd seen the movie, because Maria watched every movie and TV show she could, and read every book she could get her hands on. To learn English, she said. She already spoke better than some Shifters who'd come to America twenty years ago.

"Can Sean do his magic and find out who owns the car?" Ellison asked. He mimed typing on a keyboard. Sean could do amazing things with an old computer and dial-up modem.

"Not really," Sean himself said, coming in from where he'd been cleaning up the kitchen. "I already tried it, and got nothing on the plate numbers. They might be fake. Finding out who owns a dark blue recent-model Escalade is playing needle in a haystack. If they drove a 1952 powder-blue Chevy Fleetline DeLuxe with a dent in the right fender, I might have more luck."

"There could be another way," Dylan said.

Ellison had the feeling he knew what Dylan meant, and Sean nodded.

"You're talking about Pablo Marquez," Sean said.

"Didn't y'all run him out of town?" Ellison asked. "After he nearly got Ronan's mate killed?"

"He's been proving himself a useful man," Dylan answered in his quiet way. "He's got a stranglehold on trade coming into South Texas, and keeps the more dangerous of the lot at bay. He knows what he's doing."

High praise from Dylan Morrissey. Made sense, though, that a man like Pablo, overseer of transactions not exactly legal, would know about anyone else trying to stay under the radar in his town.

"I say we go talk to him," Ellison said.

"Aye," Sean said, a sparkle in his blue eyes. "Be good to intimidate— I mean *visit*— Pablo again."

"Agree," Ellison said. "Let's get Spike."

Maria rose from the jumble of big white toy blocks. "We'll wait for Ronan first. And then I'll come with you."

"No, you won't," Ellison said at once.

"If this Pablo knows who's trying to take Olaf, I want to ask him questions," Maria said, anger in her eyes. "I know a thing or two about people who snatch other people and take them away. I won't sit at home waiting for you to bother to tell me what's happening."

The thought of Maria anywhere near Marquez made Ellison's wolf start to snarl. "I'll tell you," he said, a growl in his voice. "I won't keep you in the dark. But you wait here—or better yet, go across and stay with Den."

Maria put her hands on her hips. "And wait how long? Besides, maybe I can ask him questions you won't think of."

"*Maria.*"

They were a foot apart, Maria's eyes holding dark fire. She was scared, but not for herself. For Olaf. For the cubs. And that gave her the strength of angels.

"Ellison and Maria were kissing," Olaf announced abruptly. He put another block on his three-foot-high robot then stood up as Sean and Dylan swung around and stared at Ellison. Olaf looked up at Maria, innocence in his dark eyes. "Maria, does that mean you're mates?"

CHAPTER SEVEN

The room went still. Maria watched Sean and Dylan fix their blue gazes on Ellison, waiting for him to respond.

Ellison went as quiet as they did. He was the outsider here, on their territory. He contrasted the Morrisseys with his gray eyes and light-colored hair, his taller body more rangy than the broader-shouldered Felines. He'd resumed his shirt, black cotton stretching over the torso that had been warm and bare in the May sunshine.

The two Felines wanted Ellison to answer, to tell them exactly what he'd been doing with Maria, the woman who was under their protection. The friendly ease in the room changed in an instant to threat and the threatened.

Maria had gone through too many tense situations between Shifters to stay calm about this one. She'd seen Miguel face off often enough against one of his lesser Shifters, looking at him the same way Dylan looked at Ellison now. Then had come violence, more fear.

She stepped in front of Ellison and bravely faced Dylan. "If I decide to kiss Ellison, it's my business."

Dylan looked past her to Ellison. "Are you making a mate-claim then?"

"I wouldn't have accepted if he had," Maria said, raising her chin. She'd decided once she'd climbed out of that basement that she'd never let anyone talk over her again. "It's only kissing."

"Maria." Ellison's voice was low and warning.

"I don't care. You all say it is the woman's choice to accept a mate-claim, and then you talk like it's decided for me. I'm not mating *anyone*."

"Maria," Ellison said again. He put a broad hand on her shoulder. "It's all right. I'm not in their pack. I'm not about to let them bully me."

"Pride," Sean corrected. "Felines have prides. Lupines have packs."

"Well, no shit," Ellison said, his drawl broad.

"That was for Maria's benefit." Sean gave her a half smile, but Maria's heart still pounded with the unspoken threats. "I like that she's choosy. Makes good sense."

Dylan alone remained silent. He was a hundred years older than the others, which made him more careful.

His gaze was for Maria now, not Ellison. Dylan had looked Maria over when she'd first been rescued, when she'd stood on a hot, dry airstrip in Mexico, understanding that she was to go away with more Shifters. Dylan's gaze had been calm, holding the weight of ages. He'd not looked at Maria in hunger, as Luis and Miguel and his Shifters had, but in watchfulness.

Now Dylan's watchfulness returned. But there was

something new in his eyes—concern for Maria, and also respect.

She saw the same in Sean. The Morrisseys had watched Maria like the overbearing father and older brothers she no longer had. She was grateful to them for it, but she would not let them browbeat her.

"Are we going to go talk to this Pablo?" she asked.

She felt Ellison tense behind her, his hand still on her shoulder. Dylan, Maria knew, would not get one step closer to her, and neither would Sean.

Dylan looked from Maria to Ellison and back to Maria again. "Yes," Dylan said, giving her a quiet nod. "Sean, fetch Spike, and we'll go."

———

Ellison's warmth felt fine on Maria's left side as he drove her in his big black pickup the short journey to speak to Mr. Marquez. Maria sat between Ellison and Spike, Spike's tattooed bulk squeezed into the cab with them. Dylan's small white pickup followed with Dylan and Sean and the Sword of the Guardian.

Spike bulged with muscle, his entire body covered with tatts, and he kept his head shaved. In the last six or so months, Spike had relaxed, changing from a man who lived for nothing but fighting to one who had more to love. Discovering he had a four-year-old cub, and finding his mate, Myka, had softened the Feline who'd once been hard as granite.

Ellison drove them to a warehouse district and a large mechanic shop housed in one of the older warehouses. When the two pickups pulled up, Spike and Ellison emerging from one truck, Sean and Dylan from the other, the guys working on cars stopped and slowly straightened. Gazes followed the four Shifters and Maria, with Sean's sword obvious on his back, as they moved toward the entrance.

The man called Pablo Marquez had an office in the back of the warehouse, shut away from the noise of the men working on cars. Pablo had dark hair and eyes, Latino coloring, wore a business suit, and rose smoothly when they came in.

He was also a criminal. Maria sensed that before she took two steps inside. He didn't shout the fact—his clothing was tasteful and he didn't flash jewelry, but she knew. He was too congenial, too courteous, and there weren't enough cars being worked on to pay for this cushy office and his thousand-dollar suit.

"I saw you coming," Pablo said, remaining on his side of the desk. "Which means you wanted me to. How are you, Dylan? Sean. Ellison." He cleared his throat as he looked up at Spike. "Eron."

Spike gave him a nod, not betraying surprise that Pablo called him by his real name. Only Myka called Spike Eron, but Pablo seemed the kind of man who knew everything.

"Drink?" Pablo asked without moving. "I have plenty of cold beer, stronger if you want it."

He carefully didn't look at Maria. Maria saw his curiosity about her, but he was acknowledging that she belonged to the Shifters, and he wouldn't poach.

Not long from now, Maria thought with conviction, *I won't be treated like a possession. By anyone. I'll stand up and tell people like Pablo Marquez what to do with them-selves.* She started to smile, imagining it.

Ellison didn't see her smile, because he was standing in front of her, a barricade between her and Pablo, but Sean shot her a puzzled look.

"What did you come to ask me to do?" Pablo said, lacing his fingers together. "And why does it take four Shifters and a civilian to ask it?"

"Ellison," Dylan said.

Ellison described what had happened in the tunnels—how he'd found Olaf about to be abducted by the three men with a net and a tranq rifle, how he'd chased them out of the culvert to see them leap into an SUV. Ellison rattled off the license number, but Pablo held up his hand.

"I don't have to look it up. High-dollar SUV, professional thugs with top-of-the-line equipment, fake plates. That's Clifford Bradley." Pablo shook his head. "He's dangerous. Very dangerous. Even for you, I think."

"If he's so dangerous, why haven't I heard of him?" Dylan asked.

"He's a recent arrival. From Atlanta, but he works the entire country. He also doesn't have his finger in things you'd be involved in—you'll never see him at the Shifter fight club or throwing back a beer at a local bar. He's high dollar. The higher the better. He has clients in New York, Los Angeles, London, Paris ..."

"Clients for what?" Dylan asked in his quiet voice.

"Drugs mostly. The very expensive kind that fund wars. Weapons. Diamonds. Anything he can move that's sought after by the ultra-rich and untouchable. I'm too small-time for him—I don't even think he knows I'm alive. Fine with me. I leave him alone."

"Why would he try to take Olaf?" Maria asked. "Not for ransom, was it?"

She knew that kidnapping was a lucrative business in some third-world countries. Even people who couldn't pay much for the return of their loved ones would manage to pay *something*.

On the other hand, though Shifters had more resources than most humans realized, they were perceived to live close to the bone. A man who dealt in diamonds might not believe he'd get much from Shifters.

Pablo spread his hands. "I've heard rumors—and I haven't heard them lately—that some very rich people like to keep captive Shifters, especially when they're young." He swallowed and looked at the Shifters, who were watching him in absolute stillness. "As pets."

Silence descended. Outside the office, the clink, clink of tools went on, a sudden clatter and a swear word in Spanish as someone dropped a wrench.

Ellison was the first to speak, his Texas drawl toned way down. "And you didn't bother to tell us this, because ...?"

"I said I hadn't heard of it happening *lately*. Last time was before I ever met you."

Dylan remained in place, standing with the utter stillness of a big cat as he watched prey play not far from him. Entirely his choice whether to remain quiet and not attack, or reach out and take down the unfortunate animal within reach. Sean stood as quietly as his father, and Maria swore she saw the sword's hilt on his back shimmer once.

Ellison and Spike were just as still. Maria stood close

enough to Ellison to hear the low growl working up in his throat. Spike's hands balled into fists, the tatts on his arms stretching, while his dark eyes pinned Marquez, who wet his lips.

Maria knew enough about Shifter encounters to know who had all the power in this room. It wasn't Marquez with his guys outside and probably weapons hidden everywhere.

Dylan ruled, with Sean, Ellison, and Spike tying for second. Marquez was at the bottom of the food chain, and Maria was neutral, an observer, and protected. If Marquez made any attempt to use her as leverage over the Shifters, he'd die quickly, and by the look on his face, he knew it.

"I want to meet this Bradley," Dylan said.

"No, you really don't," Marquez said quickly. "He has ice in his veins. He doesn't care about family, or life, or even the stuff he buys with his money. It's all about him being in control. He's ... What do you call those people with no conscience? A sociopath."

"Find out," Dylan said in a hard voice. "I want to know for certain if he's behind the attempted abduction, and where he is now, and then I will meet him. He's made a mistake."

"Yeah, I know." Pablo rubbed his forehead. "Austin's your territory. You said."

Maria had to lean around Ellison to ask her question. "What happens to the cubs when they get too big to handle?"

Pablo shrugged, looking uneasy. "I don't know. They keep them on as bodyguards, maybe as servants? I have no idea."

"You will find out," Dylan said. Not a suggestion.

Maria knew that no grown Shifter would allow him- or herself to live as a servant or bodyguard against his or her will. Even the smallest of cubs could be difficult to manage—she knew how much she struggled to make Olaf mind her, and he was one of the more docile cubs. She watched Spike chase little Jordan around Shiftertown every day, and Spike was ... Spike.

Cubs went through Transitions to adulthood at some point. Scott, another of Ronan's brood, was going through his Transition—hormones flooding his body and filling him with mating frenzy, which made him crazed and dangerous. And whenever humans thought a Shifter endangered them ...

"They kill them," Maria said, her mouth stiff. "Don't they?"

"Maybe," Pablo said.

The sword definitely shimmered that time.

Dylan fixed Pablo with a gaze that had become white blue. "Find out every single person who's bought a captured Shifter and what happened to that Shifter. I want names and locations. I want them soon."

"I don't work for you," Pablo said. "You know that, right?"

Dylan flicked his gaze up and down Pablo, and Pablo's face lost a little color.

"Do it," Dylan said. "As a favor."

"You're asking for a hell of a favor. Does that mean you'll owe me one back?"

Dylan held his gaze a moment longer then turned and walked away in silence, fading into the shadows.

Spike and Sean followed, their rigid backs betraying their barely contained rage. Ellison pivoted but remained as a shield between Maria and Pablo as he started to walk her out.

"You're Maria Ortega, am I right?" Pablo asked in Spanish.

Maria stopped. Ellison did too, turning to face Pablo but again keeping himself a protective barrier for Maria.

"Why?" Maria countered.

"You're the one they brought back from Mexico," Pablo went on, switching to English, which meant he wanted Ellison to know what they were talking about. "From the feral pack. I heard how your brother treated you when you tried to live with him. If you want, I could always explain to him that he needs to be kinder to you."

Maria thought about her brother and his old-fashioned ideas about how women should fit into the family. They were to be pure angels, married off to men of their parents' choice, to produce children to strengthen the line. A ruined woman was of no value at all, except to be unpaid help to her brothers and sisters and their children.

Maria had put up with that at her brother's house until she couldn't anymore, but that didn't mean she hated her brother. He was caught up in his own life with his wife and children, ignorant of what Maria had truly gone through. She could never make her brother understand, and she knew it.

"No," Maria said sharply.

"He's an officious little bastard," Pablo said. "I could make life very hard for him."

"No," Maria repeated. Pablo wasn't wrong about her brother, but she wouldn't wish harm on him. If she became nasty and vindictive, Miguel would have won. "Please leave him alone."

"You heard the lady," Ellison said, still standing like a pillar between Maria and Pablo. "Touch her family, and I'll make you regret it."

Pablo eyed Ellison a moment, then his severe expression softened into a grin. The smile made him go from hard-ass to almost friendly in an instant.

"Yeah, that's what I thought."

Ellison growled then ushered Maria out to the lot where Dylan and the others waited, Pablo chuckling behind them.

———

MARIA PACED BACK AND FORTH ON ELLISON'S PORCH, the breeze of her passing touching Ellison where he leaned on the porch rail. Deni had joined them, folding herself up in a porch chair, watching Maria work out her distress.

Ellison couldn't stop looking at Maria—her dark hair mussed from the ride home in the open-windowed truck, her body swaying as she walked back and forth, back and forth, her face flushed, her agitation uncontained.

"We need to do something. *I* need to do something." Maria shook out her hands as she walked. "Mr. Marquez can possibly raise an army, and so can Shifters. We go after these men *before* they hurt the cubs."

"We will go after them, sweetheart. Definitely. Dylan's in there planning things." Ellison nodded at the house across the street, to which Dylan and Sean had retreated after they'd returned, and into which Liam had disappeared a few minutes ago. Spike had all but sprinted home when they got back to Shiftertown, worried about Jordan, but he'd walked back to Dylan's house a little later. "They'll come get me, and then we'll go kick some ass."

The only reason Ellison wasn't in with the other Shifters was that he'd wanted to stick with Maria. She was too upset, too horrified. The need to comfort her, to reassure her, overrode everything else.

"I need to do something *now*," Maria said, her dark eyes flashing. "Call Pablo and ask him where we find Bradley's headquarters, and we'll go drag him out."

Ellison pushed himself away from the railing. "I'm as mad as you are, sweetheart, but I know Liam and Dylan will put together a good plan. I'll go with them, and Ronan, and we'll get this guy. Trust me."

Ellison itched to feel Bradley's throat between his hands, wanted to see fear in the man's eyes. After that, he'd explain to the three goons who'd tried to snatch Olaf why that had been a bad idea. He'd explain so hard they'd never get up again.

Killing humans was dangerous for all Shifters, as Ellison had tried to explain to Tiger, but only if the dead were obviously victims of a Shifter attack. Ellison could think of a number of ways to make it not obvious.

On the other hand, Maria wanting to rush up to Bradley and shake her fist in the man's face scared the shit out of Ellison. Maria was crazy-furious enough to try it, and then some goon would try to shoot her. Or grab her and have fun with her.

No one was touching Maria. A growl of feral rage worked up in his throat, and Ellison caught Maria's hand as she skimmed by again. "Come on."

Maria stopped, agitated. "Come on, where?"

"Somewhere you can work this off."

She blinked up at him. "We can't leave Deni alone."

Deni spoke from the shadows. "Since when? I'm not that fragile."

Deni was upset, though, not happy about what Ellison had told her. Ellison had feared that the news of Bradley kidnapping and selling cubs might trigger another of Deni's violent episodes, but she'd remained cognizant, if distressed.

Now she made a shooing motion. "Will and Jackson will be home soon. They'll take care of me. You do what you need to do."

Ellison tightened his grip on Maria's hand. "We're going."

He half dragged Maria down the porch steps to the motorcycle that waited in the driveway on the side of the house before she could think of more arguments to stop him. Technically, the motorcycle was Deni's, bought by Ellison to replace the one she'd been on when she'd wrecked, but Ellison was the only one who rode it now.

He knew exactly where to take Maria. He got her mounted behind him on the bike, warming to the way she confidently slid her arms around him, started the motorcycle, and slid it onto the street.

CHAPTER EIGHT

Ellison drove out of Shiftertown, and down to the Bastrop Highway to head east. Austin had spread in the last twenty years toward the smaller towns around it, but once past the last strip malls and housing developments, the land rolled into the Hill Country. Roads were long, miles into nothing.

A while back, while exploring out here, Ellison had found a dirt road that wound up into hills by the river, the road shielded by a spread of trees that followed the small ridge. Few came this way, a perfect place for Ellison to change to wolf and enjoy loping through woods and up and down the hills. The main roads were distant, and not many knew about this place, not even other Shifters.

Ellison drove the motorcycle out to this road now, not stopping until they were as far from civilization as they could get to in one afternoon. Under the cool shade of trees, he helped Maria off the bike, not letting go as she regained her feet.

Maria looked up at him, her hair tangled from the ride, her eyes still full of fire, stirred by anger and fear. She'd been through so much, this woman, and still she faced down the world, standing up for herself and the weaker, like Olaf.

She drew a breath to say something, but before she could, Ellison wound his arm around her, drew her up into him, and kissed her.

He tasted her agitation and outrage, and liked it. Maria's lips, dusky red and warm, moved on his, her kiss more practiced and confident than the one earlier today. She kissed in anger, seeking him, needing release.

Ellison pulled her closer, fitting her body against his, every curve of her against every hard plane of him. She was warm from the ride, mouth hot, skin damp with sweat, her scent filled with spice and heat. He could drink her all day, here away from the world. Nothing else mattered but this moment, his heart pounding desire through every space of him. Out here, Maria was his.

Maria pushed at his chest, breaking them apart, though she didn't step away. She was breathing hard, the spangled shirt that hugged her breasts rising with her breath, its little buttons beckoning his fingers.

"Why would someone do that?" she asked, rage in her eyes. "Try to take the cubs like that?"

"Bradley?" Ellison could barely remember the guy's name after that heated kiss. He barely remembered his *own* name. "For the money. And the power. But we'll teach him, darlin'. Don't you worry about that."

Maria didn't calm. "Why do people like him think they can walk into someone's life and *take* them? Away from everything? Like they own the world and can do whatever they want? They steal a person's whole life." She balled her fists. "*Why?* And why do we let them?"

"Come here." Ellison pulled her rigid body close again, knowing what she was really talking about. "You didn't *let* what happened to you happen, sweetheart. They were feral Shifters. They wanted you—they took you."

"You don't know. You weren't there. I did it to myself. I walked right into it, took my *own* life away from me. And now my family won't forgive me, and I'm alone. With no one. Just me."

"And me." Ellison let his voice go low as he stroked both hands down her back. "And what are you talking about, you did it to yourself? It wasn't your fault, honey."

"Yes, it was. I was stupid. So stupid."

Ellison smoothed her hair, letting the satin warmth of it fill something in him. "Well, once you tell me all about it, love, I'll know too. And I'll keep explaining that Shifters do whatever they want, and ferals don't even bother to be polite about it. Don't keep this inside yourself, Maria. What happened?"

"What I did made my own family turn against me. My brother didn't want me around his little girls, didn't want them influenced by me. That's the main reason I came back here. I could take it if my brother hated me, but he was teaching his kids to be afraid of me."

A red haze of anger rose in Ellison, wolf anger. "Marquez is right. You're brother's a bastard, and I'd like to explain it to him. Now, I want to hear your side of the story, so I can tell you again that it wasn't your fault."

When Maria looked up at him, the heartbreak and anguish in her eyes stabbed pain through Ellison's heart. He understood the loneliness he saw in her—he too had been ripped away from everything he knew and loved when Shifters had been discovered and rounded up twenty years ago.

He'd watched his sister lose her mate to a freak infection, and he'd watched his own parents make a pact to die together rather than submit to the Collars. He and Deni had been left alone in Colorado, bewildered, with Deni's two little cubs to take care of.

"I fell in love," Maria said, tears of anger in her voice. "No, it wasn't love. I didn't understand what I was feeling. Luis was a stranger, exciting, handsome. And I fell for his lies."

"Luis was the Shifter who kidnapped you, right? And took you to Miguel?"

Dylan had told Ellison what he'd pried out of Maria—that a wolf Shifter had abducted Maria to add to the pack at Miguel's instigation. But Dylan had given Ellison only cursory details, and only after Ellison had badgered him. He'd wanted to know everything about Maria.

"I didn't know Luis was a Shifter, not until later," Maria said. "I was a stupid girl, bored with being a good daughter and with waiting to marry the right man. Luis convinced me to run away with him. And I did it. Because I'm an *idiota*."

The tears finally came. She didn't sob uncontrollably, but beads of tears formed on her lashes then splashed quietly to her cheeks.

"And the asshat Luis turned you over to Miguel." Ellison's anger made his voice harsher than he meant.

"I didn't understand what he wanted. I thought Luis was taking me to a big house, where he would marry me. But then he revealed he was a Shifter, and he took me to the abandoned warehouse. When I saw the other Shifters, I was scared and tried to run away. But they dragged me down into the basement and said I had to stay there with the female Shifters. They locked us in."

Dylan had pretty much related all this, but hearing it in Maria's halting words made Ellison's anger escalate to furnace-level rage. A spark snapped in his Collar, warning, and he stepped away from Maria, the wolf in him ready to kill.

"My family might have forgiven me if I'd been abducted," Maria said. "But I walked away from them. I went with Luis in the middle of the night, and then I thought he'd protect me."

"Maria. Sweetheart." Ellison took a breath, trying to cool himself down, but he was finding it hard.

She didn't need a Shifter going kill-crazy in front of her, but Ellison fought the instincts that made him want to race away and find Miguel *now*.

"You *didn't* go of your own free will, so stop saying you did," he said. "Shifters know how to coerce. Trust me, I've lived with them the past hundred years. They do what they want, Collared or no, and these were crazy-ass ferals. You might have walked out of your house on your own two feet, but you didn't go of your own free will, sweetheart. But even if you had, Luis should have protected you. That's what mates *do*. They protect you from all others. Every evil in the world. He didn't do what he was supposed to." And for that, Ellison wanted to taste his blood.

"Luis did try to protect me." Maria wiped the tears from her face. "Miguel killed him when he tried. And Miguel killed Luis's cub before that, or as good as—he let the cub die. *My* cub."

"Goddess." Ellison's Collar flashed another spark, but his rage negated the pain. "Maria."

In the wild, males who headed a pack or clan sometimes killed the offspring of the other males, but that practice had died out years ago as Shifters became less barbaric, and also realized they needed diverse blood to survive.

The instinct to kill a rival's offspring, though, was still there. In a community of Shifters going feral—losing every bit of compassion they had and letting themselves be driven by the needs of the beast—the instinct to kill another's cubs would be strong.

Ellison hadn't known until now that Maria had lost a cub. She'd never spoken of it, and Dylan hadn't mentioned it —maybe Maria had kept it from everyone. But Ellison should have known from the emptiness in her eyes.

"After that, I didn't care anymore what he did to me," Maria said. "I spent my time planning how I would kill Miguel and escape, but before I could, Cassidy and Diego came and blew up the warehouse. And Dylan brought me here."

Where Maria had been floating ever since, trying to make a life for herself. She now lived in the protection of Shiftertown, in a house with four strong Shifters and a cub, but Maria was alone, and she knew it.

The unmated male Shifters had been told to keep their distance from her, but Shifters like Broderick were tired of keeping their distance, and Broderick wasn't the only one.

He and others would swoop soon, and Challenges would come thick and fast. Liam would be forced to tell Maria to choose a mate to keep the peace or go live somewhere else.

Ellison would never let that happen.

He wrapped his arms around her again and pulled her in for an embrace. Shifters needed touch for reassurance, for comfort, and humans, Ellison had discovered, pretty much did too, even if some pretended not to. Maria was stiff, shaking, and Ellison held her tightly against him, not letting her go.

It was hot out here, but Ellison rubbed his warmth into her anyway, hands smoothing her thin shirt, kneading her back. He felt her start to relax into him, but not enough. She was hurting, oceans of pain, and it would take a lot of loving to ease that.

Maria looked up at him, her eyes glistening with tears, her eyelashes damp. Ellison kissed a tear from the corner of her eye then he leaned to kiss her lips.

Her mouth opened under his, her kiss hungry, needy. Ellison tasted her sadness—a mother's loss, Maria's fury, her despair—and the will that drove her to live.

The length of her body moved with his as she kissed him, her breasts soft against his chest. She had strength and gentleness rolled into one package.

Maria pulled away from the kiss, her beautiful face wet. "I'm sorry," she said. "I'm sorry. I can't ..." She wiped her eyes.

Ellison's breath came fast, his lips tingling from the frenzied kiss. "What the hell are you apologizing for?"

"I don't know. I don't trust what I think anymore."

"You've been through hell, Maria. No one can think

straight after that. I don't care if it was a year ago. But you can trust *me*."

"Trust you for what?"

"To take care of you." He caught her hand, kissed her fingers, and laid his hand and hers over her heart. "Be my mate," he said swiftly. "Let me protect you."

The look she gave him was stricken. "You don't have to. I've already decided what I'm going to do."

"Go to school, yeah, I know. You can do that and be my mate at the same time. My sister loves you, my nephews think you're cool, and everyone in Shiftertown likes you."

She nodded and looked away. "Everyone has been good to me, yes."

"Let me be better. Come on, sweetheart. All the pretty ones get snapped up before I have a chance. This time, I'm cutting everyone else out."

"Ellison ..."

She was scared. Terrified from what had happened to her before. She'd trusted the wolf Luis, and he'd not been able to save her from the worst. Trusting again would not come easy for her.

"It's not the same now," Ellison said. "When I mate-claim you, when we're joined under sun and moon, no one will get to you. Not Broderick, not anyone. I'll be your protector, your first line of defense. And believe me, I'll be a way better fighter than your Luis ever was. I'd never let *anything* happen to you. This, I promise."

SHE WANTED IT. MARIA FELT THE PULL, THE NEED TO lay her head on Ellison's shoulder and let him take her hurting away. His gray eyes were focused on her, unyielding, resolute, his body warm from himself and the Texas sunshine. He hadn't worn his cowboy hat while they rode, stuffing it into the saddlebag instead, and his short hair was ruffled by the wind and gleamed gold. He was a delicious sight.

But Maria had woken up one morning months ago, after many weeks of not wanting to get out of bed at all, realizing that the person who needed to take care of Maria was Maria. Hence her plan to go to school, get a professional degree, find a job, and live in safety the rest of her life.

Becoming a mate of a Shifter had no part in that plan. Never again.

Then again, this was Ellison. With Luis, Maria had been not much older than a schoolgirl, and she'd believed Luis was a dream come true. She'd wanted to get away from her dull life, of routine that would last forever. Luis had been handsome, romantic, a means of escape.

Ellison was a friend. The first time Maria had seen him, when Dylan had brought her straight from Mexico to Shiftertown, she was broken and barely able to speak. Ellison had made her want to laugh even then. He'd been so-over-the-top Texan—with his boots, hat, huge belt buckle, the Texas drawl, the *ma'am*. He'd touched his finger to his hat and called her that, nodding and smiling, his gray eyes warm.

Dylan had intimidated her almost as much as Miguel had, and she'd been afraid that her situation hadn't improved. But Ellison had made Maria laugh from day one—he'd been truly funny, instead of using humor to be derisive and cruel. While she'd not been able to look up at Spike, or even Ronan, she'd raised her head and let Ellison's smile make her feel better.

His smile still made her feel better, and his kisses were even better than that.

Maria reached up and smoothed his hair, liking the wiry silk of it. Ellison's eyes flickered, the Shifter in him responding, but he only closed his eyes briefly, letting her touch.

He didn't want to scare her. From the time she'd met him, Ellison had been trying to calm and reassure her, and to keep others from frightening her. He'd been right there when the asshat human had tried to intimidate her last night; he'd been at her side the moment Broderick had tried to harass her on her way home.

Now he stood in silence, letting her touch him, not grabbing her or coercing her. She ran her hands up his forearms, feeling every muscle, finding the hollows inside the bend of his elbows, the hard strength of his biceps under his shirt-sleeves. Up to his shoulders, which held the responsibility of his sister, his nephews, Deni's violent episodes.

So strong, and yet carrying so much for others.

Maria's touch went to his face, the rough of unshaved whiskers, the warm satin of his lips. She rose on her tiptoes and pressed a kiss to those lips, while he watched her, his gaze intent. One arm came around her, solid, holding her upright. The strength of him took her breath away.

And Ellison was sexy. The way he danced to the country tunes at Liam's bar revealed his grace. She felt it now as he held her without effort as she kissed him.

Maria had never touched a man like this. Her experience with sex had been limited to Luis deciding when, where, and how. Luis done all of the touching, and that hadn't been much.

Ellison was different. He caressed her back, easing her closer, kissed her lower lip then the corner of her mouth.

"I think I'm liking this kissing thing," he said.

"Me too."

Ellison touched his forehead to hers. "I'm not going to mate-claim you right now. Much as I want to. I told Broderick to give you a little space, and I will too. What I'm going to do instead is teach you how to love life."

Maria looked up at him in confusion. "I do like my life now. It's much, much better here than it's ever been."

"No, sweetheart, you're only surviving. Maybe basic surviving is a little easier now, but you're still living in the shadow of all that pain and fear. You want to go to school because—why? It will help you survive better?"

She shook her head. "I want to be a doctor, to take care of people. I can live anywhere if I do that, maybe go back to Mexico and help people who don't have anyone. Or find people here that need the same thing."

"You're kindhearted. But it's still surviving. What you mean is you want a way to take care of yourself, so you don't live under someone else's thumb ever again. Not Shifters, not family, not friends, not anyone."

He understood. Ellison's eyes sparkled gray in the sunlight and were full of knowledge. How he knew exactly what went on in her heart Maria wasn't sure, but he did.

Maria's voice was quiet. "I never want to be enslaved again."

"Neither do I." Ellison's hand went to his Collar. "You

know what Shifters know—what we've learned? That it's not enough only to survive. We want to *live*."

"I want to live too. That's all I've ever wanted. But when I tried, I nearly destroyed myself." Maria drew a breath, stifled a new wash of tears that threatened to flow. "So now I'm happy with survival."

"No you're not. But I tell you what, love, any other woman who'd been through what you have would be dead by now, or maybe in constant therapy on happy drugs. You're strong, one of the strongest women I know. Now let me teach you how to use that strength, to grab on to life and make it yours."

She wanted to believe him. Ellison's eyes sparkled with liveliness, the man more *alive* than anyone she knew.

"How?"

Ellison seized her hand in a strong grip, and grinned. It was a wide, warm grin, as big as Texas.

"Come on with me, sweetheart, and I'll show you."

———

THEY RODE. ELLISON ZOOMED THE MOTORCYCLE DOWN another back highway, the road a black line to the horizon.

Maria threw her head back and let the wind catch her hair. It was warm, the early May heat full of the promise of summer. Fields rushed by, green hills rolling from the river as the Colorado snaked eastward to the Gulf.

After about thirty miles or so, Ellison dove off the highway to another twisting dusty road that led down to the river bottoms, stretches of it overhung with trees. Ellison slowed, and Maria rested her head against his shoulder, ducking low branches and the black swarms of bugs that the little hollows bred.

They came off the winding road to a narrow lane, and a small trailer house set up on cement blocks, under the overhang of stooping trees. The tiny lane ended at this house, and the man standing in front of it with a shotgun.

CHAPTER NINE

Ellison halted the bike a respectful distance away and held up his hands. "Peace, Granger. It's only me."

"Ellison?" The man uncocked and lowered the shotgun, shaking his head. "Shit, you should have called first. I was about to blow your head off."

"Didn't know I was coming." Ellison shut down the bike and tilted it a little so Maria could slide off. He settled the motorcycle in place, pulled his hat out of the saddlebag, and took Maria's hand. "This is my friend, Maria. How's the water?"

The man called Granger chuckled. "Nice." His hair hung in a long dark ponytail, his face bore a coating of unshaved whiskers, and his full-muscled arms were covered with tattoos. His eyes, now that they weren't glittering over the barrel of the shotgun, were full of good humor.

"Water?" Maria asked.

"Swimming hole." Ellison winked at her. "Come on."

Granger shouldered the shotgun. "You kids enjoy your-selves, now."

Maria gave Granger a polite smile as Ellison led her past him. "It is nice to meet you."

"Likewise," Granger said.

Ellison led Maria into the trees, pushing aside branches for her, taking her down a steep hill. At the bottom, a wide pond, formed by a rivulet snaking from the main river, spread like a sheet of silver, sparkling under the sun.

The banks of the small lake ran up into the trees, and clumps of bluebonnets spread across every open, sunny space. Birds skimmed across the far side of the water, a wading bird turning its head to watch them approach.

Maria, having grown up in arid lands, always marveled that water could simply *be*. The life water gave—the birds, trees, wildflowers, tall grasses—constantly amazed her. The heat and humidity under the trees had perspiration dripping down her face, but she looked around with wonder.

"Where are we?" she asked.

"Don't really know. I found this place when I was running as wolf one day. Granger tried to shoot me, I dodged the blast and knocked him down, and we became friends. He knows I need the space to run sometimes, and he keeps people away when I do. He's a good guy."

Maria thought about Granger's tattoos, which Spike had taught her about this past year. She suspected Granger had gotten some of them in prison, but she said nothing.

"It's a beautiful place."

"Sure is." Ellison hung his hat on the limb of a bush that stuck out from the trees. He unbuttoned his shirt and shrugged it off, hanging it next to the hat. "Don't always see the bluebonnets either. You need the right amount of rain, the right amount of sunshine. We got lucky."

He wore a tight black T-shirt, which he also shucked, then he got out of his boots. Sunlight touched the liquid warmth of his skin and the butter-colored highlights in his hair.

"You joining me?" he asked. "I'm not swimming alone."

"Swim? In there?"

Flashes came to Maria of herself as a tiny child, her grandparents taking her to a lake in the mountains, beautiful and cool. She'd splashed around and played, while they spread a picnic lunch of all her favorite foods. Maria had thought she'd never be happier in her life. Come to think of it, she never had been.

Ellison unhooked his belt buckle and skimmed the belt from his jeans. "I don't see you getting undressed."

Maria swallowed. "You're going to swim in there naked?"

"Sure. Get my clothes wet if I don't."

"There will be snakes." The lake in the mountains had been home to plenty of snakes, and so had the warehouse, but Maria had learned at an early age how to avoid them.

"Probably. I'll scare them away."

Ellison unbuttoned and unzipped his jeans and pulled them off, hanging them carefully next to his shirts. His loose boxers came off right after that.

Maria sucked in a breath. She'd seen plenty of Shifters naked, including Ellison—they saw no shame in it, and after shifting, they took their time sliding back into clothes, as though forgetting they needed to. Shifters were casual about nudity, and Maria had stopped noticing them a long time ago.

But Ellison was difficult not to notice. His body had been touched by God, sculpted muscle under skin that moved with liquid grace. The silver and black Collar around his neck only drew attention to the bareness of the rest of his body.

He folded his arms and watched her, all that rippling strength becoming still, waiting. Ellison was a being of sunlight and shadow, but with a hint of the moon in his gray eyes.

Maria wanted to look her fill, to feast her senses on his beauty. She couldn't *not* look at his cock, hanging thick and full between his legs, dark blond hair at its base.

"*Ungh*" was the only thing that came out of her mouth.

"Come on," Ellison said. "I'm getting hot standing here."

Maria's face heated. He wanted her to strip as naked as he was and then jump into the water with him. A slow smile spread over his face, and her body flushed as hot as her cheeks.

Bareness to her meant vulnerability, fear. She hesitated, heart pounding.

"I told you," Ellison said. "I'm teaching you to live life." He came out of his watchful stance and stepped to her, his body filling her world. "Every bit of it, sucking up every drop."

His hand went to the top of her shirt and undid the two small buttons there. Polite of him, because he could have just yanked the shirt off over her head. And he did, but at least he unbuttoned it so the shirt with its pretty design didn't tear.

Maria stood in her lacy bra that Andrea had bought for

her, hugging her arms across her chest. Her low-riding jeans suddenly felt too low.

Ellison came closer. The heat from his body touched her like sunshine. He smelled of musk and dust, sweat and warmth. He slid his hands to her waist and popped open the button of her jeans.

A shiver began deep inside her. Fire rose in Maria's body, slowly surging until it blotted out fear, panic, shame. Need eased through her, tangled with warmth and desire.

Ellison's fingers brushed her abdomen as he felt for the zipper. He tugged it down, more touches to her skin. At the same time, he leaned down and kissed her.

A slow kiss, no more frenzy. Ellison's mouth was all that was good, his lips easing hers open. His tongue slid inside, a flicker, as he skimmed his hands up her back to open her thin bra.

Maria's shiver deepened as she felt the bra loosen. Fetters coming off, freeing her.

Ellison traced across her now-bare back, though he didn't pull the bra the rest of the way off. His touch went around her shoulders, up to her jaw. "Come on and swim with me."

Maria swallowed, licking the taste of Ellison from her lips. "Be right there."

He smiled, slow and fine. Another touch to her chin, and he turned away.

His bare backside was taut, legs lean and strong. Ellison unhooked his cowboy hat from the branch, setting it on his head to complete the devastating picture.

He grinned over his shoulder at her. "Last one in's a rotten egg."

Maria suddenly wanted to laugh. *What in the world did that mean?*

Ellison ran forward, jumped, caught another overhanging tree limb, swung himself out over the water, and dropped in with a magnificent splash.

His hat went flying. Ellison surfaced, swiped his hair out of his face, laughed, and grabbed the hat when it floated past.

"Come on, darlin'!"

Maria didn't give herself time to think. She toed off her sandals, slid out of her jeans, tossed aside her underwear, and ran at the water, whooping all the way.

MARIA LANDED IN THE WATER A FEW YARDS FROM Ellison, coming up with her black hair wet. She pushed the hair from her face and opened her eyes, teeth flashing in her big smile.

Ellison made himself start breathing again. He'd sucked in air and held it while her body had come into view, sweet and lush, breasts high and firm, a brush of dark hair between her legs. She'd spread her arms to run in, as though embracing the pond, embracing the world.

The water now hid everything but her lovely face and dark hair, her eyes sparkling like the waters around her.

"Whoo!" she yelled again, and slapped the surface. "I feel like a little child."

"You're supposed to." Ellison swam to her, his hat firmly on his head. He knew it was stupid to swim with his hat, but Maria liked it, so the hat stayed.

Cool water slid under Ellison's arms, twining around his

legs as he kicked his way to her. Maria hopped in a circle, taking in the banks, trees, bluebonnets, and the sheet of water. Her head and neck showed above the surface, her hair floating.

Ellison neared her, took off his hat, and sprang high enough out of the water to hang it on an overhanging limb. As he came down, he wrapped his arms around Maria.

Her body floated up to his, breasts moving against his chest in a waft of softness. Her hair was heavy with water over his hands, her lips wet as he drew her up to him to kiss them.

Kissing was the best thing. Ellison rarely kissed, because any Shifter women he'd had the pleasure of bedding had been frenzied and interested in getting the job done. Human women were few and far between. In fact, in the last couple years, anything female had been few and far between.

And now Maria. Maybe the Goddess had made sure all the women who'd ventured to Shiftertown recently—Kim and Andrea, Elizabeth and Myka—had found mates in other Shifters so Ellison would be free when Maria came along. He'd joked that he was never fast enough off the mark, but none of them had touched his heart like Maria.

The Goddess had been good to Ellison. Maria tasted like fire, of woman and wanting.

But she was hurt, like a broken bird, like Deni, who was fighting to regain her life. So much had been taken from Maria, and Ellison wanted to give it back to her, without pain, without fear.

Ellison kissed the corners of her mouth, tasting sweetness. Water droplets lingered on her lips, his tongue finding every one.

Her plump mouth was softness itself. Her lips met Ellison's, her kisses falling on the whiskers above his top lip, the curve of the bottom one.

Maria drew back and gazed at him face-to-face, her smiles gone. Ellison smoothed her hair from her forehead, the laughter leaving him as well. He read desire in her, and also terror so harsh it cut.

He'd have to be slow with her. It might take months, or years, of teaching her that he cared. That he'd never hurt her.

"Maria ..."

"Shh." Maria touched her fingers to his lips.

She kissed him again, resting her arms on his shoulders. He felt her feet leave the bottom of the lake, she balancing on him so she could let her legs come up.

Ellison forced himself to stand easy, though he caught her around the waist, steadying her so she wouldn't slip under the water. He had to let her decide what to do.

Keeping her gaze on him, Maria laced her legs around Ellison's hips, letting his cock, which was hard and vigilant, brush her. It slid between her thighs, seeking her warmth, but Ellison held back. He was on fire, but he couldn't rush her.

He smoothed his hands down her back, satin skin with a little indentation where her bra strap had been. She'd be beautiful in a sarong, one piece of clothing wrapped around her, as Shifter women liked to wear in the summer. One piece, which could come off with the tug of a string.

Maria closed her eyes as she kissed him, then she broke the kiss and looked straight at him. Her eyes were dark like velvet night, the lashes black and thick.

She brushed a lock of Ellison's hair from his forehead,

then she adjusted herself on him and slid down onto his cock before Ellison could stop her.

Sensation after sensation poured through his shaking body. Maria was tight against him, her intake of breath loud in the stillness, her eyes widening.

"Maria, sweetheart." His voice was a choked whisper.

She touched his face. "I want this."

"You sure?"

Ellison wanted to hold on, to drive into her in his growing frenzy, to spill his seed and slake his need. A Shifter was built to mate. Nature drove them to sex, to have cubs, to live as hard as they could.

But Maria was shaken and upset, and Ellison couldn't take advantage of her. He told his body that with everything he had, but he still couldn't withdraw, stop her, take her away from here.

"I'm sure." Maria brushed a light kiss to his lips. "With you. Do *you* want it?"

"You think I don't?" Ellison's thoughts started to jumble. "I need to be good to you. I don't want to hurt you."

Maria slid farther down onto him, scattering the last of his thoughts into incoherency. "You won't," she said.

Ellison felt like fire. Need crawled through him, his blood hot and his skin chilled. The water took Maria's weight, making her light in his arms.

He wanted to drive into her, not stopping until he found his deepest pleasure. He wanted to rock into her, fast, faster, find her, know her, feel her close around him, squeezing him.

But Ellison held back. He'd go slow, he'd show her caring, tenderness.

If he *could* hold back. Maria's legs were silken against his tight skin, the depths of her like a wash of flame. Ellison pressed higher into her, holding on, his arms shaking. His toes curled as he braced himself in the mud at the bottom of the little lake, the bluebonnets all around them shimmering in the warm breeze.

"Ellison," Maria said in her low-pitched, and damn sexy, voice. She licked his cheek, hot tongue chasing water droplets. "I need you."

Father God, help me.

The sun, the Father God's symbol, seemed to laugh, kissing Ellison's shoulders with heat. *A blessing,* something inside him whispered. The sunlight, the cool water, this woman in his arms.

Ellison slowly thrust up inside her. She squeezed instinctively, embracing him inside her as she embraced him in her arms.

The sensation rocketed through Ellison's body, engendering another thrust. Up and up again, the water buoying him. Maria kissed his cheek, then across his cheekbone to his ear to nibble his lobe.

It was erotic and tender at the same time. Maria was opening to him when she'd been terrified and closed for so long.

A gift. And Ellison was glad to receive it.

He thrust again, holding her, making love to a beautiful woman in the sunshine. The water cradled them, her breasts crushed to his chest, and she brought her caressing mouth to his lips.

This kiss was slower, less tense, the warm goodness of two people sharing the ultimate intimacy.

Ellison rocked carefully into her. Her body welcomed

him, accepted him, held him and didn't let go. He couldn't move as much as he wanted in this position, but it didn't matter. This was their bodies getting to know each other, becoming one.

He'd spill his seed soon. Too soon. Ellison wanted to stay inside Maria forever, closer to her than he ever dreamed he could be.

"Goddess, you're beautiful," he said. "You're the most beautiful thing I ever saw."

He brushed her face with his lips, kissing her eyelids, her cheek, the corner of her mouth. Ellison licked across her cheekbone, then returned to her mouth, sliding his tongue inside as the first of his shudders hit him.

Maria was feeling it too, he knew, her eyes half closed, little sounds of pleasure drifting from her throat. She kissed him back as her body moved with his, her hips rocking to pull him farther inside her.

"*Damn.*" Ellison released, control leaving him. Joy poured over him, every piece of his body aching with pleasure.

It was beautiful. *She* was beautiful. The sun flushed Maria's face, and her eyes were warm, her body welcoming. The Goddess had made her for Ellison, and Maria was embracing him and taking him. Ellison needed her in his life the same way he needed air every second of the day.

Maria gave a little cry, Ellison thrusting now in crazed need. He kissed her, she kissed him, they struggled to hold each other in the slippery water.

"Ellison," she said, her voice stricken.

Ellison held her close. "Shh," he said. "Shh, love." He

shivered with release. But he was hot too, inside himself, where they joined, and wherever she touched him.

"Shh," he said again. Maria kissed his cheek, the kiss languid, and Ellison gathered her and held her close.

———

ELLISON CARRIED HER OUT OF THE WATER. MARIA trembled in reaction to her impulsive decision to make love to him and the sudden cold of the breeze on her wet skin.

Ellison set her on her feet on the bank, wrapped his big body around her to cut the chill, and kissed her.

All the heat of the spring day poured from the kiss into her. Maria warmed, though she still shivered. She wanted to stay here forever in this beauty, this feeling.

Fear was gone. She had Ellison, passion, this flood of happiness. She wanted to hold the moment, swathe herself in it, and never leave for the real world again.

Ellison caressed her cheek, his kiss slow with lassitude and lovemaking. His body was as wet as Maria's, but his skin held so much warmth, hotter than any living being's should be.

I'm falling in love with you. The thought came to her unbidden, as natural as the breeze that ruffled the lake. *I'm falling in love with you, Ellison.*

He lifted her hand to his mouth and kissed the backs of her fingers. A cloud slid over the sun, and Maria's shaking increased.

"We'd best get you dressed," Ellison said.

He looked up at the tree from which he'd hung their

clothes, and started laughing. Next to his jeans, a couple of blankets dangled in the breeze.

"Good old Granger. Don't worry, he didn't look."

Still chuckling, Ellison yanked down one of the blankets and folded it around Maria. The scratchy wool smelled of smoke and outdoors, but it cut the wind.

When they were dry, they dressed again. Ellison looked at Maria plenty as she pulled clothes over her damp body, and she didn't pretend not to look at him. He grinned at her again as he picked up his hat, but he didn't set it on his still-wet hair.

The sun was setting by the time they reached the trailer, the long spring day drawing to a close. Granger had a small fire going in his front yard, and was poking at it with a long stick. He invited them in, and Ellison took Maria's hand and led her into the trailer.

Inside was small but cozy. Granger was a bachelor, obviously—no woman's touch in the cluttered interior. Maria sank down on the seat under the window, and Ellison was beside her. His arms went around her, drawing her back into his warm body.

Maria started to drift off to sleep. The smoke from the fire held a strange, sweet odor, the trailer was comfortable, and afterglow from lovemaking made her want to lie here with Ellison and never get up.

Ellison slid his thumb under her jaw and turned her face to his. His kiss was slow, hot, holding the same afterglow.

Granger came noisily in. Ellison broke the kiss and cradled Maria back against him, and she started drifting off again.

"You're gonna get yourself arrested," she heard Ellison say, humor in his voice.

"Nah. The sheriff's deputies around here are my best customers. Hey, I have some errands to run. You guys hang out here as long as you want, and leave when you're ready. There's beer in the fridge and some food. I forget what."

"Sure." Ellison's voice rumbled in his chest.

Maria snuggled up to that rumble. In the pond, she'd given in to her desires, and she didn't regret it one bit. In the water, so close to the strong, caring Ellison, she'd put away fear and acted on new feelings.

Ellison had been tender, gentle, taking it easy. She'd felt him shaking, holding back his incredible strength for her. He hadn't wanted to hurt her or scare her.

Now he held her safely against the darkening day ... No, the dark. The window was black now, the fire burned out, and only a weak light shone in the corner of the room.

Maria should get home. Tomorrow, Connor was to pick her up early and drive her to where she'd take her SATs. She had to be ready.

No, she had to stay here with Ellison. He'd get her home and to bed in time. It was nice to lean on someone, to have him hold her and keep all the bad things away.

Except that he was gone. Maria woke fully to find herself alone in the trailer, the door moving on its hinges. The light was out, the night was impenetrably dark, and Ellison wasn't there.

CHAPTER TEN

Maria got herself up off the bench. She was out in the middle of nowhere, inside a trailer belonging to a man she'd never met before today, and the Shifter protecting her was gone. Ellison might trust this Granger, but who knew what the man could or would do? Maria wasn't given to trust as easily as—well, anyone.

She softly opened the door and stepped outside. Moonlight filtered through the trees and filled the little clearing with white light. The fire had died to a tiny glow, and the smoke had gone, leaving the air clean and fresh.

Maria's thoughts were much clearer now too. She needed to find Ellison and get back to Shiftertown. She had to know what Liam and Dylan were planning to go after the man trying to abduct their cubs, and she wanted to be part of it. Ellison had been right to bring her out here to cool her down, but her concern for the cubs' safety rose.

But where to look for him? If she went blundering around in the dark, she'd get lost or maybe fall into the lake or something. Plus snakes would be everywhere. Texas crawled with rattlesnakes, especially after dusk, when they came out of their holes to soak up the last of the day's warmth. In spring hordes of baby rattlers joined them.

Maria sank down onto the front steps and pulled her feet up under her, in case snakes decided to come out from under the house and investigate her ankles. She had her cell phone, but a peek at it told her she was out of range of the rest of the world.

What was she doing? The cubs could be in trouble, and on top of that, she was supposed to take her SAT tests tomorrow. How on earth could she concentrate on those between worry for the cubs and running off into the wilderness with Ellison?

The trouble was, she'd felt more alive today than she had in many, many years—since that day at the lake with her grandparents.

What filled her mind was Ellison, the memory of him pressing inside her, spreading her, breaking apart her defenses. She could still feel his hands hot on her back, his strength holding her, the hard plane of his chest against her breasts. He'd been hard and hot, deep inside her, the feeling glorious.

She'd feared sex, which before had hurt whenever she'd felt anything at all. She'd climbed upon Ellison in a moment of daring, her fears laughing at her.

And now Maria couldn't stop thinking of him. The wild burst of pleasure, the joy of watching his face soften with passion, the water holding them—these things would mark her forever.

A step, nearly soundless, but audible in the stillness,

made her raise her head. Maria studied the line of trees circling the trailer, but she saw nothing.

She stared hard at the place from which she thought she heard the noise. The sound came again, barely a whisper of movement against grass.

Then a huge gray wolf stepped out of the woods into the clearing. Moonlight brushed his fur with silver, outlining his large, lithe body and pricked ears. He turned his face to her, his eyes as silver as the moonlight, then he looked away, scanning the woods as Maria had done.

The wolf turned his steps to the trailer, picking his way in silence across the ground, blending into the shadows. He halted when he reached Maria and sank to his haunches beside the narrow steps.

He was huge even sitting down, his body nearly twice the size of a wild wolf's. Maria wasn't afraid. The wolf was beautiful, though she knew he was deadly, but all that deadliness now protected *her*.

Maria stroked his back, shivering at the wild strength of him. His fur was wiry and soft at the same time, and held heat and comfort.

"Everything all right out there?" she whispered.

Ellison turned from scanning the woods and nuzzled her, rubbing his furry face against hers. Then he licked her.

"*Ay*," she said, laughing softly. "No wolf spit."

He made a rumble like laughter. Ellison scanned the woods again, nose working as he tested for scent. Then he rose to his feet and transformed himself with a crackle of bone and flesh to Ellison.

Naked Ellison, towering above Maria, his scent full of spice. The night was warm, sultry, back here in the woods near the lake, the air heavy and damp. It seemed right to be here, alone in this strange place, with only a Shifter to protect her, because that Shifter was Ellison.

Her friend. Her champion. And now, her lover.

Ellison sank down to sit next to Maria on the edge of the step, unworried about his nakedness. He braced his hand behind her, a well-muscled arm against her shoulder.

"We should go." His paused. "Damn, you don't know how much I did not want to say that."

"I don't want to leave either."

They sat in silence a moment, a cool breeze brushing the clearing. Crickets and frogs took that as a cue to start singing for the night.

Ellison let out a sigh. "You got your test tomorrow, right? And I'm not easy about Bradley and his goons. I want you safe."

"He's abducting Shifter cubs, not small human women," Maria said.

"Yeah, but he knows you take care of Shifter cubs," Ellison countered. "His guys were waiting for Olaf today, knowing you'd go that way. That wasn't coincidence. They were following you."

Maria shivered. "I figured that. You're right, we should go."

Ellison's eyes flashed in what was left of the firelight. They were Shifter eyes, the lightest gray, full of wildness. "Like I said, I don't really want to." His voice held a growl. "I want to stay here, kick out Granger, and hole up with you for as long as I can. I want to claim you, and mate with you, and keep you away from all others. That's the Shifter in me—

don't matter about Collars and being civilized and all the rest of it."

The declaration should frighten her. Miguel had captured females then sequestered them and used them when he saw fit, telling the other males in the pack to do the same.

But Maria understood, after living in Austin these past months, that Luis and Miguel had been anomalies. Most Shifter males cherished their mates. She'd seen the women in Shiftertown happy—deliriously so—smiling at their mates, slow-dancing with them at the bar, loving how enclosed they were in their families.

Luis should have taken Maria away and protected her instead of subjecting her to the danger of Miguel and the other the feral Shifters. Miguel too should have made sure his mates were well taken care of, not miserable prisoners.

Maria had seen how Ellison cared for his sister, keeping her from harm, and how stridently he prevented Maria from being harassed by Broderick and other Shifters who called her fair game. Ellison had protected Maria at every turn, and asked for nothing from her.

Maria put her hand in his broad one. She ran her thumb over the back of his hand. "I'll go back with you."

Ellison closed a hard hand over hers. He said nothing, only looked at her, his chest rising with a sharp breath.

Maria rose and kissed him, letting the kiss linger on his mouth. "With you," she repeated. "It's only ever been you."

Ellison tightened his grip on her hand, fingers biting down, and exhaled. "Thank you."

———

Maria expected to slip unnoticed into the dark and silent house across from Ellison's after kissing him goodnight, but she walked into her bedroom to find Andrea sitting on her bed, waiting for her.

Andrea had Kenny in her arms, the boy with his tuft of unruly black hair sleeping soundly in the crook of Andrea's arm.

"*Worried sick*, I think, is the term," Andrea said, her gray eyes watchful in the light Maria turned on. Those eyes narrowed as Andrea inhaled. "Ah."

Andrea's Shifter nose would smell Ellison all over Maria. Maria slipped off her shoes. "You didn't need to worry at all."

Andrea gave her a nod. "You go well together. Ellison is one of the good guys." She said it with confidence, no doubts that the mating would go through.

"Was everything all right here?" Maria asked. She came to Andrea and brushed her hand over the sleeping Kenny's hair. "No threats to cubs?"

"No." Andrea rocked her son, who slept the limp sleep of an infant secure in his mother's arms. "The cubs are safe in Shiftertown. No one gets in that we don't know about. No one will take them from here."

"But you can't keep them holed up here forever." Maria stroked Kenny's hair again, the down soft on her fingers. "They can't be imprisoned, even if it's for their own safety. That isn't right."

Andrea's look softened. "We'll always be closed off from the rest of the world in some ways. We're Shifters, Maria. People fear us. We'll always be apart. But we manage together." She smiled. "I should know. I'm half Fae. That has most of Shiftertown still a little wigged out. I'm apart even from other Shifters."

Andrea's Fae blood had never bothered Maria, and she still wasn't certain what being Fae meant. But she'd observed Shifters glance at Andrea with curiosity and even fear. They never said anything, knowing Sean would retaliate against any disrespect to his mate, but the nervousness was there.

"I'm apart too," Maria said. "But I decided I can't hide forever. There's a world out there, and I need to face it. It's a risk, but I will take it."

"And you will. Tomorrow. Your SAT tests. I hope you didn't forget." She smiled, knowing Maria never would. Maria had confided in few people about her dream to enter the university, but Andrea was one of them. She and Connor, Glory, and now Ellison.

"What did Dylan decide to do?" Maria asked. "About Bradley?"

Andrea's look turned evasive. "They'll stop him. Dylan, Liam, and Sean together. No need for you to worry about that."

"Yes, but how? Find the man? Murder him? What happens if they get caught?" Maria looked at Kenny, sleeping so sweetly. The boy had been named for the brother of Sean and Liam who'd been killed by a feral Shifter long ago. Kenny had been Connor's father and much beloved.

A shadow passed through Andrea's eyes, worry for her mate and his family. "If there's a problem in the world Sean, Liam, and Dylan can't take care of, then it's a *bad* problem. Don't worry."

"We have to stop them, Andrea—these people who

snatch cubs. Bradley and everyone like him, and the people who hire them. It's terrible."

"I know." Andrea held Kenny closer a moment, protective. Then she handed Kenny up to Maria's outstretched hands and rose, stretching as only a Shifter could stretch, every limb supple. She kissed Maria on the cheek. "But you focus on your tests tomorrow. It will be a big day for you."

Maria enjoyed the warmth of Andrea's hug for a moment, the baby scent of little Kenny. Andrea took Kenny back into her arms, left the room, and Maria turned out the light.

She went to the window and raised the blind enough to let in the moonlight. On the porch across the street, two cowboy boots were crossed on the porch rail, long legs in jeans stretching back into shadows.

Maria smiled, her heart lightened. She undressed, blew a kiss across the street, and got into bed, where she lay awake for a long time.

Thoughts tumbled through her mind—the panic when she's lost Olaf, her sudden fright inside the culvert, her rage when she discovered that men were trying to kidnap Shifter cubs, the distracting worry about the exams.

Over all of this she relived the water embracing her, Ellison holding her, the heat of him inside her, finding something buried deep inside her and dragging it out into the light.

After a long time, she drifted to sleep to the memory of the warmth of Ellison's touch, the tenderness of his kiss. The image of him running into the water, naked but for his cowboy hat, was a fine one too.

"Here, I found more pencils for you." Olaf held them up on the porch in the early light of morning, yellow pencils nicely sharpened.

Elizabeth—Ronan's mate—and Cherie, Scott, and Rebecca, another Kodiak bear, were with Olaf, Ronan hulking in the background while he talked to Spike and the Morrisseys.

"Thank you, Olaf," Maria said, taking the pencils and putting them into her purse.

"Why did you get up early to take a *test*?" Jordan, Spike's four-year-old cub, asked her. "That's no fun."

"You should write the answers on your hands," Scott said. A large bear Shifter of about thirty years, he seemed calm this morning, not in the frenzy of his Transition. "Always worked for me."

"It's not that kind of test," Maria said, laughing. "I think they check for that anyway."

"Aw. Too bad." Scott grinned.

"I still don't see why she has to go," Jordan said. "Stay home and play with me, Maria."

Connor, who was waiting impatiently at the bottom of the porch steps, said to Jordan, "You'll understand when you're older, laddie. We need to go."

Difficult to leave when all of Shiftertown—at least this block—had turned out to see her off. Maria had talked about her ambitions to very few, but this morning, so many seemed to know her secret, and they were excited for her. Hard to keep anything quiet in Shiftertown. Maria warmed though, at the send-off.

Spike's mate, Myka, a human woman who trained horses for a living, was also making an early start. Horses liked early, she said. She hugged Maria. "You'll bust chops," she said. "That means you'll do well."

Glory almost lifted Maria off her feet with her hug. "You go, girl. I'm so proud of you."

Andrea had another hug, and this time Kenny was awake and talking to himself in wordless sounds. Maria kissed both him and Andrea.

That made Olaf and Jordan clamor for kisses and hugs before she went. Maria bent down to hug each in turn, having to pry them away from her and promise more hugs when she came home.

The only Shifter missing was Ellison. She kept glancing at his closed house, but she heard nothing from within. Maybe Ellison had simply gone inside and fallen asleep after staying up all night watching her house from his porch. He had to sleep sometime.

Maria swallowed her disappointment and turned to follow Connor to Dylan's pickup, which she and Connor were borrowing. Tiger was tinkering with something under the hood, and he dropped the hood closed, watching Maria quietly with his strange eyes when she and Connor approached.

Ellison still didn't appear as Maria took the keys from Connor and got into the driver's side of the truck.

"You know, I do know how to drive," Connor said, hopping into the passenger seat.

"I know. I've ridden with you. I want to get there in one piece."

Maria looked behind her, but Ellison's house remained

quiet, the doors closed. Well, she would go over when she came home. She and Ellison weren't mates or married. Just friends.

And lovers. Maria shivered as the heat of yesterday afternoon slid over her again. She started the truck, smiled at Tiger, who returned her look without changing expression, and pulled onto the street.

Behind her the Morrisseys, Ronan's family, and Spike's family all waved and cheered for her. A warmth spread in Maria's heart. She'd been trying so hard to survive on her own that she hadn't realized she'd created a family for herself right here, without knowing it.

"Test me while we go," Maria said to Connor.

Connor unfolded the sample book he'd had ready in his hands, and started asking her questions. Maria had chosen to take one of the biology subject tests. She'd studied and studied, with Connor's help, for the last six months. She'd learned so much—knew the sample tests back and forth—but knots formed in her stomach. What if she went blank when the actual test lay in front of her? What if she couldn't remember *anything*?

She shouldn't have let Ellison take her out yesterday. She should have broken away from him and shut herself in the house. She was tired now, and so distracted by thoughts of Ellison, bare in the water ...

"I said, what is found in DNA but not RNA?" Connor asked. "Is it, a) ... "

"Um. Thymine. Right?"

"Yes, right. Concentrate."

"I'm trying."

Connor shook his head as he turned the page. "That's

what mating frenzy does to you. Clouds your brain to everything but mating. At least, that's what I hear. I won't have that joy for a few years yet."

"I don't have mating frenzy," Maria said firmly. "I'm not a Shifter."

"But you had sex with Ellison, you can't stop thinking about it, and you want to do it again. That's mating frenzy."

Maria clutched the steering wheel. "Who told you that? Why can't Shifters mind their own business?"

"Well, that would be boring, wouldn't it, now?" Connor grinned over at her. "And it's true, isn't it? You didn't have to tell me anything. Scent doesn't lie."

Andrea had known too, right away. Maria heaved a sigh. "If I admit that yes, I had sex with Ellison, will you stop talking about it?"

"Nah." Connor laughed. "It's fun to see you blush. So what about it? Ellison's dying for a mate. Sun and moon, eh? We're loving all the mating ceremonies around here. Nice excuse to get drunk and party."

"*Connor*. I have to take my test this morning. Can we talk about mating later?"

"Sure. Next question ..."

Fortunately, the drive to the school that was administering the test didn't take long. Maria parked in the front parking lot, her stomach knotting even more. Connor got out of the truck with her and gave her a long hug.

"You'll do great. And I'll be right here to pour you back into the truck when you're done and take you home. Or out for a drink. I remember when I finished my SATs. I was all wound up, and I wanted to sleep for a week."

"Thanks, Connor." Maria returned the hug. Connor had

dark hair and blue eyes like his uncles and grandfather, his body already filling out to their formidable bulks. Girls liked to stare at him, and when Connor finished his Transition years from now, he was going to be in high demand. "You've helped me so much."

"Hey, we have to stick together. I'm not old enough to take my place in the hierarchy yet, so who knows where I fit in? You're trying to figure out your place too. That makes us automatic friends."

He pulled Maria close for another hard embrace. Reassurance, comfort—Shifters knew how to give it. Maria hugged him back, grateful for his unconditional acceptance.

Finally Connor released her, patted her shoulder, and held out his hand. "Cell phone."

Maria turned it over. Cell phones and the like weren't allowed at the test. She had to go alone with her testing device, calculator, and the pencils Olaf had given her. Connor pocketed the phone, clasped Maria's shoulder again, and sent her off toward the building with a little shove.

Maria looked back as she walked down the curved sidewalk. Connor had climbed into the bed of the truck, leaning back with his feet up, to read a newspaper. He'd wait for her. He'd be here, her anchor.

The kids who'd come to take the test this Saturday morning were all about ten years younger than Maria, excepting a few adults who, like her, were hoping to go to college for the first time. It cost money, but there were ways to find it and people who would help. Maria had explored every avenue and put together a plan to combine scholarship opportunities with working. It would be tough, but she would do it.

An air of anticipation hung over the building Maria entered. She checked in, following the directions to the room where she'd take her test. Kids who knew each other talked excitedly, hiding their nervousness, while others found seats, eyes wide with anticipation.

The current of anxiousness was palpable. Maybe Maria had lived with Shifters too long, because she picked up every nuance of worry, fear, and excitement.

She chose a desk near windows that overlooked the parking lot. Maria could see Connor lounging in the truck fifty yards from her, the sight of him reassuring. Connor had been such a help to her ever since she arrived. She couldn't imagine surviving this long in Shiftertown without Connor. Or Ellison.

Ellison. No, Maria needed to focus. She'd suck it up, do the test, and then relax on Dylan's porch with her friends, and let thoughts of a bare Ellison run through her head all she wanted. He'd been beautiful as his wolf, his fur itself quivering with his strength. She'd loved stroking him ...

"You may start," the man who was proctoring the test said.

Maria jumped, watery fear running through her, and opened the test booklet. She looked at the first question with numb eyes, and let out her breath again.

She knew that one. She could do this.

Maria answered a few more questions with confidence, then looked up and out the window to reassure herself with Connor's presence again.

And saw him slumped over in the truck, his body limp. She also saw two men she didn't recognize climb into the front of the truck and drive it away.

CHAPTER ELEVEN

<hr>

Maria jumped out of her seat. The other test-takers looked up and around in irritation.

"You need to sit down," the proctor said.

Maria remained standing, watching the truck speed up and out of the parking lot. She turned around, blindly afraid, and made for the door.

"You can't leave until the break," the proctor said, rising and following her.

"I have to. This is an emergency."

The man looked annoyed. "If you leave the room, you'll need to turn in your test and forfeit your fee."

Meaning she'd have reschedule the test for who knew when and save up more money for the fee. But someone was busy abducting Connor, and all thoughts of tests, university, and the rest of her life went away.

"Sorry," she said. She shoved her incomplete test at the proctor and ran out of the room.

Outside she stared at the parking lot from which Connor

had disappeared in dismay. He had her cell phone, and she was in a building whose offices were shut up for the day, and the campus was deserted, everyone here today focused on testing. The proctor might have a phone she could borrow, but he'd decidedly locked the door after she'd run out. She needed a phone and needed it now.

An ordinary person might have given up. But Maria had grown up in a tiny town with few luxuries in the middle of a desert, and she'd learned to be resourceful. She started jogging down the street, heart in her throat, wishing Ellison was with her, and knowing she needed to find him.

———

ELLISON HELD DOWN HIS SISTER'S WOLF, GROWLING AT her. He was dominant. She needed to *obey*.

Deni snarled and fought. She'd woken up out of a bad dream this morning, confused and forgetful again. She'd charged out of her room in wolf form, attacking Ellison as soon as he'd walked in the front door after standing guard over Maria all night.

Deni and Ellison had fought a silent battle on the floor for a long time before Deni had suddenly gone limp, giving up. Ellison had carried her back to bed and turned to get dressed again to go with Maria and Connor to where she'd take her test, only to discover that Deni had been playing possum.

As soon as Ellison turned to leave Deni's bedroom, Deni had come out of the bed and leapt onto his back. He'd heard Connor and Maria drive away while he'd fought off several hundred pounds of wolf.

Will and Jackson had already left for the day, their jobs starting at first light. Ellison and Deni battled it out alone, she too strong and swift to give him time to call for help.

Ellison pinned her with his large wolf's body, Deni swiping with claws and teeth, a mad light in her eyes. Both their Collars snapped sparks, the pain biting Ellison deeply.

This was insane. And heartbreaking. One day Deni would go too far and seriously injure Ellison or her own cubs, or Ellison would have no choice but to kill her.

The idea sent a wash of pain through him at the same time he staved off her attack, she trying to rip out her older brother's throat.

The phone pealed into the rumble of growls and snarls. Deni jerked, her attention diverted, but Ellison didn't dare let go of her to answer it.

He knew, though he didn't know how, that the person on the other end was in danger. Jackson and Will were out there, neither wanting to stay home from jobs they liked. Connor was out there too, with Maria.

Ellison tried to get up. Deni used his distraction to attack, jaws open, fangs bared.

Ellison caught her as he shifted, hands digging into her fur, swung her around, and threw her across the room.

Deni tumbled, howling, and crashed into the wall. Before she could get herself up again, Ellison dove for the phone.

"Ellison." He heard Maria's panting relief, and his fears skyrocketed.

"Where are you?" he said, his voice guttural. "What's wrong?"

"Connor. I couldn't stop them. I was taking my stupid

test. He was waiting in the parking lot for me because I was nervous."

"Wait. Stop. Tell me."

Maria drew a long breath and told him in simple words what had happened. "I'm at a convenience store at Congress and Ben White. What are we going to do? We have to *find* him."

"You stay right where you are. I'm on this. Aw, *shit*."

Deni crashed into him, yanking the landline phone out of the wall. The phone went dead, Maria's voice vanishing.

Deni's eyes were red, the feral in her taking over. Her Collar shocked more sparks deep into her, but the pain didn't slow her down.

They fought out of the kitchen and to the living room, Ellison trying desperately to stop her. He'd have to knock her out somehow and get away from her. Connor needed help *now*.

The back door banged open. Ronan charged in, already throwing off his clothes, and became a giant Kodiak bear before he hit the living room.

Seriously hit it—the doorframe broke and a table full of Deni's knickknacks went over. Deni rolled away from Ellison and faced this new threat.

Ronan roared, a colossus enraged. Deni laid her ears back and bared her teeth, ready to fight. Her stance told Ellison that she expected her brother to join her in beating back the intruding bear.

Ronan raised a paw to knock her senseless. Ellison jumped at him, instinctively defending his sister, his pack.

Ellison's leap ended on Ronan's massive paw. The Kodiak tried to pull his punch, but the blow smacked Ellison head over tail to land him on the couch. The couch broke into a pile of wood and stuffing, Ellison's wolf buried in the debris.

In that moment, sanity flooded back into Deni's eyes. She rose and flowed back into human form, her face ashen. "Ellison!"

She rushed to Ellison and put her arms around him, stroking his fur, while Ellison lay stunned, trying to catch his breath. Ronan subsided, watching them both anxiously.

"I did it again, didn't I?" Deni asked, her voice broken. "Ellison, what are we going to do?"

The question was a serious one. Shifters who went mad, and who were aware of their madness, sometimes took what they thought was the easiest way out for themselves and their families.

Deni's hopeless look worried Ellison. At the same time ... Connor.

Ronan shifted back to his human form, a huge, muscle-bound, naked man. "Sorry, Ellison. You OK?"

Ellison climbed out of the ruined couch, shaking foam rubber out of his fur. Deni rose to her feet, finally noticing the overturned table and broken door. Her expression turned to dismay. *"Ronan."*

Ronan flushed. "Hey, I said I was sorry. I'll fix it. I promise. We need Ellison though. Right now."

"Why?" Deni fell into the nearest chair, folding her arms across her stomach. "What happened?"

Ellison shifted back to human form. "Connor's been taken," he said grimly.

Deni leapt to her feet again, her strength returning. "Oh, Goddess. By that Bradley guy?"

"How did you find out?" Ellison asked Ronan. "He contact you?"

"Maria did. She called Sean when your phone went dead. Sean sent me over here to find out what was up with you."

"Goddess," Deni said again, stricken. "Go, Ellison. Find him. I'll be fine."

"Come with us," Ronan said to her. "We might need you."

Deni hesitated, which made Ellison's heart churn again. A few short months ago, Deni would be the first out the door, ready to fight. It wasn't like his sister to hold back.

"What if I ..."

"Go insane on the kidnappers' heads?" Ellison asked. "I'm not worried about it. Come on, Den. What if they had Jackson or Will?"

Deni's eyes went flat. "Let them try."

"Good girl."

"Hurry," Ronan said as he grabbed his clothes. "Dylan's waiting, and Liam. They're ready for war."

"Go with them," Ellison said to Deni. He caught his sister in a rough hug then released her. "I'm not coming. I need to find Maria."

Ronan looked worried. "Do I have to tell Dylan that?"

"*I'll* tell him," Deni said. "Ellison's right. Maria will be terrified, and Ellison can't leave his mate stranded. Dylan will have to suck it up."

Ronan ushered Deni, who was pulling on her sweats, out the door. "I dare you to say *suck it up* to Dylan."

"He understands about mates and cubs. They come first."

Ellison dressed as quickly as he could then headed for his motorcycle. Deni, back to herself again, herded Ronan across the street, and Ellison's blood warmed in spite of his worry.

Mates. Deni had recognized the mate bond when she saw it. Ellison knew, that after all this time and so much loneliness, the mate of his heart had found her way to him.

———

MARIA'S RELIEF WHEN ELLISON DISMOUNTED HIS motorcycle in front of the convenience store made her knees weak. Maria dashed to him, and in an instant, his strong arms were around her, Ellison sweeping her up into his warmth. Maria buried her face in his neck and hung on.

"You all right?" Ellison asked.

"Yes, yes, *I'm* fine. Connor ... It was awful. They just took him!"

"I know. We're on it."

"But why take him? He's a cub, but not in human terms, not like Olaf."

Ellison went silent, and Maria raised her head to find his gray eyes troubled. "I admit, I don't know. But we'll find him."

His expression was somber, but his arms were strong around her. So good to be able to lay her head on his shoulder, for him to understand her burdens, to share them, to fight with her.

"Hey!" A voice sounded across the convenience store's tiny parking lot. "Shifters aren't allowed here."

Maria turned around, hot words on her lips, but Ellison stopped her. "Never mind. Let's go hunt for Connor."

Maria clamped her mouth shut. She didn't like the convenience store clerk's sneering expression, but now was not the time to fight this battle. After they found Connor, she'd come back here and say rude things to him.

Ellison helped her onto the back of the motorcycle. As she had only yesterday, Maria wrapped her arms around him and let him carry her away.

She realized after Ellison had made a few turns away from the convenience store that they were not going back to Shiftertown. He rode them down to the warehouse area they'd visited yesterday morning, with its empty back lots that might as well be in the middle of nowhere.

Ellison stopped in the open space in front of Pablo Marquez's warehouse. Guys working on two high-end cars gave Maria and Ellison warning looks as they left the bike and went inside.

Pablo Marquez sat at his desk in his office, tapping a laptop's keyboard. "I already talked to Dylan," he said before Ellison reached him. "I don't know where they took Connor, but I suggested some leads. You can go away now. I'm busy."

Ellison walked steadily to the desk and stopped in front of it, doing nothing but standing there. "You know where Clifford Bradley is," he said. "Don't you?"

CHAPTER TWELVE

Pablo made himself not blink. Shifters liked to stare a man down, to intimidate with a steady gaze. Pablo had learned in this last year that showing fear was the worst thing he could do—no matter that the small boy he used to be was quivering inside him in terror.

"Don't mess with Bradley," Pablo said. "Find the cub and then go home. I'm telling you this for your own good."

Ellison leaned his fists on Pablo's desk. "You're working for him, aren't you?"

"No." That was the honest truth. Bradley wasn't paying him.

The wolf Shifter inhaled sharply, testing Pablo's scent, hunting for lies. "But you know," Ellison said. "Tell me everything."

Pablo had always thought of Dylan as the scary one. He knew damn well that at any time, for any reason—or for no reason at all—Dylan could simply kill him and walk away.

He had no illusions that the human police would be very bothered about Pablo's death, and Dylan knew that too.

Ellison was different. He was the most laid-back of the trackers, with his cowboy hat and his slow West Texas–style drawl. He, Spike, and Sean did little more than stand as silent pillars behind Dylan when Dylan came to visit, although Ellison might toss in an understated joke or tip his hat on the way out.

Today Ellison had left his hat behind, and the Texas drawl was laced with steel.

Pablo contrasted Ellison in his jeans and button-down shirt with Bradley and his ice-cold eyes and five-thousand-dollar suits. Bradley was dangerous because he was all business, no sentiment. The man had no family, no friends, no warmth in him whatsoever. The Shifters would lose against him, because they were *all* warmth, all emotion. Bradley was a robot.

"If I tell you, I'll get you killed," Pablo said.

The human woman, the cute little thing called Maria, stepped forward. From what Pablo had seen, she was a smart, compact firecracker. If he were fifteen years younger and not in love with his obnoxious, silken-haired hacker girlfriend, he might think about her for himself. But the way Ellison closed in on her protectively told him that, nope, she was spoken for.

"Mr. Marquez," she began. That was sweet, calling him *Mr.* "Think about this. If it was your brother, your son, or your best friend who was missing, what would you do? You'd stop at nothing to go after Mr. Bradley, wouldn't you? You are that kind of person."

"True," Pablo said. "I'd go find Bradley and get my head taken off for my trouble."

"You're not Shifter," Maria said. "Shifters can do amazing things."

"I don't doubt it." Pablo turned the force of his gaze on her, and met brown eyes full of fire. "You want to see him shot down?" He gestured to Ellison. "With enough firepower to blow him to pieces right in front of you? Bradley and his boys are used to dealing with Shifters. I mean, shit, he steals their cubs."

"Which is why you're going to help us," Maria said. "He took Connor, *while I was watching*. Do you know what that made me feel like?"

"Yeah. Actually, I do." As a teenager, Pablo had seen his best friend dragged off by a rival gang and executed, while he'd hidden in terror, unable to do anything to stop it. From that day to this, he'd vowed to have the power to never have to go through that again. He'd protect his family and friends to his last breath. "I do get it. But sweetheart, let Dylan and his crew handle finding Connor. You go back home and wait."

Ellison spoke again, the accent not as pronounced this time. "Bradley wouldn't have taken Connor to his own house. He'd have a place to stash him until delivery, and that's where you sent Dylan and Liam. Right? What I want is Bradley himself. The body of the hydra. Not its heads."

"Cut one off, two grow back, right?" It had been a long time since Pablo had read a book, but he remembered that story. "Let it go, man. Dylan will obliterate the thugs who did the kidnapping, you'll have the cub back safe and sound, and all your Shifter friends will live."

"And it will happen again," Ellison said. "And again."

"Cubs will have to imprison themselves in Shiftertown," Maria said. "We can't let that happen. *I* won't let that happen. I thought you were a tough guy, Mr. Marquez. Why haven't you eliminated your competition?"

"Because Bradley's not competition. And I don't have a death wish."

"You're a criminal," Maria said. "I'm sure you'd like it if you could remake those stolen cars outside without being bothered. If you help get rid of someone like Bradley, just think how much the cops around here will appreciate you."

"Just think how much every other gang boss *won't* appreciate me. They'll never trust me again. I'll be a dead man walking." Sweat beaded on Pablo's forehead. He didn't want to have to kill Ellison and Maria, because he liked them, but these two were getting crazy.

"No, no," Maria said. "You'll be a hero. I bet your rivals aren't thrilled with Bradley either. I bet you all have to pay *him*, not the other way around."

She really was too smart. "You know, sweetheart, I like it here," Pablo said. "Austin's a cool town. Great music scene, awesome food. Something for everyone. I don't want to have to leave. Understand?"

"Maybe you won't have to." Maria smiled.

Now Ellison was looking at Maria as though he wanted to yank her out of here and hole her up somewhere safe. Poor guy would have his hands full with her.

"Tell us where he is, and then you can sit here and work on whatever it is you're doing," Maria said. "Otherwise, we'll come back with Ronan and Spike and all the others, plus every cop in town. Maybe some reporters too. That would be fun."

"Don't threaten me, sweetie," Pablo said in a mild voice. "You won't make it out the door."

Ellison didn't move, but Pablo saw the wolf gleam in his eyes. One of Ellison's fists tightened minutely on the desk. "Tell us." Ellison's voice was a touch too soft. "No one needs to know where the information came from."

"Right. Shifters visit me, then Shifters go after Bradley. They'll know. Then Bradley steps over your broken bodies and comes after me."

Ellison's fist went even tighter. "You won't have to worry about that. But if you don't help now, you'll have to worry about me. And Ronan. And Spike. That's just for starters. I won't talk about Dylan and Sean, and you don't even want to know what Liam will do to you. The rest of us are Girl Scouts compared with Liam. He's the alpha of the alphas. He does what he has to do, no matter what."

Damn it. Pablo had known when his little brother had stupidly gotten Shifters pissed off at them last year that he'd would never get out from under them. He could toss them at Bradley and rid himself of his Shifter problem, but he knew it wouldn't be that easy.

"I don't know," he said. "My girlfriend's niece is a Girl Scout, and they can be pretty vicious when it's cookie time. I always end up buying about fifty boxes."

"I'm sure your men appreciate that," Ellison said, straight-faced. "You give up Bradley before I lose my cool, or you'll wish you were facing an army of little cookie-selling girls in green."

Maria watched Pablo, not Ellison. Pablo held out a moment longer, then one of the most powerful eaders in South Texas bent his head, sighed, and said, "I'll see what I can do."

———

SHIFTERTOWN WAS NEARLY EMPTY WHEN ELLISON AND Maria pulled into Ellison's driveway. Ellison helped Maria off the bike, then he walked her across the street to Dylan's house, to find the door locked.

Andrea answered Ellison's knock, looking tense. "I thought you'd be with Dylan and Sean," Andrea said as she let them in. Locking doors was unusual in Shiftertown, and Ellison hoped this wasn't the beginning of a trend.

"Took a detour," Ellison said. He looked around the quiet house. Kenny was sleeping in a bassinet, Liam's daughter, Katriona, playing by herself in a playpen. "Where did they go?"

"I don't know. Sean said he'd keep me posted when he could, but he hasn't checked in yet. Which means he can't. Kim went to talk to the police."

Ellison returned to the porch and looked up and down the empty street. "Leaving Shiftertown deserted when someone's kidnapping cubs isn't the best idea."

"They didn't. Ronan is still here. He's scared for Olaf and Cherie. Broderick is here too, because he won't leave his younger brothers and nephews. And Tiger. Liam wouldn't take him—too afraid he can't control him. Tiger is livid, which is why I've got the kids. I'm not leaving them or this house."

"Good. Maria … " Ellison slid his arms around her and leaned down for a brief kiss.

The brief kiss turned into something deep and hot. Ellison felt Andrea's gaze on them as he eased back, but he enclosed Maria in a tight hug.

"Stay here with Andrea until it's safe. And thank you for alerting us. They sure knew how to pick the right moment."

Maria's dark eyes glittered as her brows came down. "I wasn't about to sit and finish my exam when Connor was in danger. I can always take another test."

"I know." Ellison kissed her forehead. "That's why I love you."

He turned away, pretending to ignore Andrea's interested look, left the house, and started across the street.

Maria banged out the screen door and followed him. He should have known she wouldn't stay put.

"You don't think I'm letting you go after Mr. Bradley by yourself, do you?" she demanded as she caught up to him.

"Yes, I do," Ellison said, not turning around. "You're not Shifter. You can't fight."

"You also didn't wait for me to answer," Maria said as Ellison let himself in his front door with his key. Deni had locked up too.

"Answer what?" Ellison tossed his keys to the table and sniffed, scenting that no one was home. He needed to call Jackson and Will, make sure they were still safely at their jobs.

"That I love you too," Maria said.

CHAPTER THIRTEEN

E llison's body went so still that Maria barely saw his intake of breath.

She'd known he'd thrown out the *That's why I love you,* offhand, Ellison always joking.

But he had murder in his eyes, rage so deep that he wouldn't stop to think before he attacked Mr. Bradley.

Maria knew that Pablo wasn't wrong to say that Bradley was untouchable. She might not have another chance to tell Ellison what she felt.

"What?" Ellison asked, his voice deadly quiet.

"You heard me."

Maria started to push past him into the house. Ellison clamped a hand on her shoulder, drawing her back, turning her around. She looked up into gray eyes that held hunger and silent need.

"I know I heard you," he said. "I want you to say it again. Like you mean it."

"I do mean it."

Ellison's eyelids slid down in a slow blink. When he opened his eyes again, they were lighter gray, the wolf in him coming out. "Say it again, Maria."

Why not? She wasn't ashamed or afraid. Maria drew herself up straight and looked into his eyes. "I think I love you, Ellison Rowe."

His fingers bit down. "You *think?* What, you're not sure?"

"I don't know what real love feels like. I loved my parents and grandparents, but I was a child. I thought I loved Luis, but I never really knew him." She swallowed under Ellison's burning gaze. "All I know is, I can no longer imagine my life without you in it."

Ellison yanked her against him, his hands remaining on her shoulders. His grip held raw power—strength, but not imprisonment. Never that.

"Then mate with me," he said, his voice low, savage. "Let me mate-claim you, and join with me sun and moon. I'll give you ... everything."

Maria warmed against his body. "Will you stay alive for me? And stay with me?"

Ellison started to smile. "You bet. But I hope you're not gonna ask me to stay home and not go after Bradley."

"No." Maria said. "I want you to get that sucker. We need to, as Spike would say, take him down."

Ellison's eyes narrowed. "Who's *we?* You are staying with Andrea."

"We need to stop him, Ellison," she said.

Ellison stilled again, the laid-back human with the smiles and jokes fading into the Shifter who took care of his family at any cost. "We will. But not with you. I don't want him knowing anything about you."

"He already does. Like you said, he had his men following me with the cubs, and he knew Connor went with me to the test today. He must have planned the abduction by watching me, figuring I wouldn't be able to stop anyone taking Connor."

"Yeah, but to Bradley right now, you're just the human female who lives with Shifters. He's an idiot if he thinks you're nonessential, but I want him to think that, if it means he'll ignore you. You flash yourself in front of him, he'll have you in his sights as a person trying to interfere with his lucrative business."

"If you're so confident you can stop him, it won't matter." Maria balled her fists. "We have to stop him, Ellison. They can't keep trying to hurt us."

Ellison's eyes flickered slightly, and Maria realized she'd said *us*.

Well, she *was* one of them now. She'd lived with the Austin Shifters, laughed with them, helped take care of them, and loved them, for months now. Ellison had imprinted himself on her, and she knew that no matter what else she'd do in life, she'd somehow be bound to him.

"We will stop Bradley," Ellison said, a deadly edge to his voice. "But my way."

"Fine, but I will be with you every step of that way." As Ellison started to turn from her, Maria put herself in front of him. "You know that if you go without me, I'll find a way to follow. Unless you intend to lock me in the basement?"

"No." Ellison's tone was harsh. "I'd never do that." He'd never be like Miguel, he was saying. Never imprisoning her.

Never. Then he grinned. "Although, there's a new flat-screen TV down there. Doesn't have cable, but Sean rigged up a way to get us internet."

Maria's eyes widened into a glare. "Are we going or not?"

"Yep." Ellison gripped her shoulder again. "I'm taking you, because I know that if I don't, you'll follow me, and I can't be worried about where you are. So you'll stay with me, and when I tell you to keep out of sight, you do it, all right?"

"Of course I will. I don't have teeth and claws, or a handy weapon, so what could I do?" She looked up at him in all innocence.

Ellison gave her another suspicious look, but he nodded, as though he accepted her words. "Fine. Let's go get backup."

———

BACKUP MEANT, FIRST, RONAN, WHO DIDN'T WANT TO come. "Ellison," Ronan said, standing in his front door and filling the entire doorframe. "What if they're waiting for us to empty Shiftertown? Then they come in for the rest of our cubs?"

Olaf peeked out from behind Ronan, and Ellison was aware of Scott and Rebecca in the background. Ellison seethed with impatience.

"An attack on Shiftertown is a different thing from their snatch-and-grab modus," he said. "Rebecca won't let anything happen to the cubs—you know that."

"You got that right," Rebecca said. She was tall, like most Shifter women, but when she shifted to her Kodiak bear, in all of Shiftertown, only Ronan was bigger.

"And I'm not chopped liver," Scott said. "Anyone comes for Cherie and Olaf, and I'll let my craziness come out."

"We need you Ronan," Ellison said.

"And if he's too much of a wuss to go," a voice said behind Ellison. "I'm game."

Broderick. The wolf Shifter stood on the walk between Ronan's house and converted garage, arms folded. "I know you think I'm an asshole," Broderick said before Ellison could speak. "But I have nephews and younger brothers. We cut this off at the source, Ronan."

Ronan stroked Olaf's hair, pushed the lad gently behind him, and closed the door. "Fine. I'm coming." He glared at Broderick. "But I'm going at you at the next fight club. For calling me a wuss."

Broderick looked pained—no one won fights against Ronan, except maybe Dylan. But at least Ronan was coming.

"Can we hurry?" Maria asked, as impatient as Ellison.

"One more," Ellison said.

He'd saved the best for last. He knew that once Tiger joined them, the man wouldn't want to slow down to let Ellison pick up anyone else.

When Andrea unlocked the door for them to Liam and Kim's house, Tiger was nowhere in sight. Ellison scented him, though, and the Tiger-man was not happy.

"He's downstairs," Andrea said. "Comfortable with TV and lots of snacks. Liam didn't want him following."

Ellison faltered a step. "You mean Liam locked him in there?"

"Yes. The basement door's reinforced steel. The only thing that would hold him." Andrea smiled her half-Fae, half-wolf smile and dangled a key from its ring. "Here you go. I'll be at home."

She got herself out of there with amazing swiftness, the back door slamming. Ellison heard her run back to her own house, the cries of Katriona and Kenny welcoming her.

Ellison grasped the key and drew a breath. "Everyone needs to clear a space. Maybe you should all leave the house."

"Nope," Ronan said. "If he attacks, you need us to help pull him off you."

Maria, at least, had the sense to leave the kitchen. She ducked out of the big room to the living room beyond. "Good luck," she said.

Gee, thanks. Ellison approached the door to the basement, tucked near a broom closet in the back of the kitchen, squared his shoulders, and put the key into the lock.

As soon as the key turned, Tiger slammed into the door from the other side, nearly tearing it from its hinges. Ellison had danced aside, knowing what was coming. The door, made to withstand Shifter strength and police battering rams, remained whole, but only just.

Tiger roared and leapt at the first Shifter he saw—Broderick.

"Shit!" Broderick yelled, his feet coming off the floor as Tiger's entire body hit him.

"Tiger!"

The cry came not from Ronan but Maria. Tiger paid no attention. He slammed Broderick into the wall, shoving him halfway to the ceiling.

Ronan and Ellison gripped Tiger on either side and tried

to haul him back. Broderick screamed and fought, his half beast emerging in defense.

Maria put herself where she could look into Tiger's crazed face. "Tiger!" she shouted again. "We need you. And Broderick. Do you want the man who captured Connor?"

Tiger halted. He swiveled his yellow gaze to Maria, fixing on her. He stared at her for a few more heartbeats, then he dropped Broderick to the floor and stepped over his prostrate form.

"We get him."

Maria patted Tiger on the arm. Instead of jerking away, Tiger accepted the caress, and then carefully sniffed in her direction. "Mate-claimed," he said, and looked at Ellison.

Broderick climbed from the kitchen floor, accepting Ronan's hand up. "What? Oh, you bastard."

"Challenge me," Ellison said. "*Please*. I'm going to need to work off some steam."

"Later," Ronan growled. "We need to go."

"Yeah, I Challenge," Broderick said. He had his hands on his knees, trying to catch his breath. "In front of witnesses. Eat it, Ellison."

"Fight club," Ellison said. As the Challenged, it was his right to name time and place. "Tonight."

Broderick stared. "Are you nuts? We don't know what will go down today."

"If we survive, fight club. Done?"

"Shit." Broderick gave him a nod. "All right. Done."

Ellison laughed. His fighting blood was up. He was in love, he'd made love with the most beautiful woman in the world yesterday, and she'd told him she loved him today.

The most beautiful woman in the world started yelling at

him in Spanish. Ellison understood only a few words, like *idiota*, but he laughed again. Maria was fiery, she was courageous, and she was his.

Now to find Bradley, kick his ass, kick Broderick's ass, and take Maria into his arms again.

———

"I can't believe you talked me into this," Pablo said from beside Maria in Ellison's truck.

"Insurance," Ellison said, his voice rumbling pleasantly from Maria's other side as he drove. "In case you decided to go behind us and tell Bradley we were coming."

"Would I do that?" Pablo sounded innocent.

"You would totally do that." Ellison grinned across at him, his drawl becoming pronounced. "So you come with us, my friend."

"And you're bringing your girlfriend? You Shifters are insane."

"Yeah, we are," Ellison said. "No telling what we'll do next."

He stepped on the gas of his black pickup, shooting them down the highway past Bastrop and out into the country. A big fire had devastated this area not long ago, destroying homes in and around the historic little town. Shifters from Austin and the Hill Country Shiftertowns had gone out to help people evacuate and save what they could, though that detail hadn't been made public.

No one had heard from Dylan or Sean about the search for Connor, and none of the Shifters dared make a call in case a stray cell phone ring endangered the Morrisseys.

Maria's heart was cold with fear for them, but she knew they *would* call if they had news. They must be searching, planning what to do—or in the middle of a fight for their lives. Not knowing was hard.

Pablo had said that Bradley had a house east of Bastrop on the river, an estate that encompassed about a hundred acres, surrounded by a fence and a large electronic gate. Bradley didn't do his business there, Pablo said—he conducted business in offices and warehouses around the city. He didn't piss in his own sandbox.

Maria found the phrase strange but apt. If police raided Bradley's house, they'd likely find nothing. Pablo's information, though, meant that Connor probably wouldn't be at the house either.

Ellison drove with one hand, while Maria held Pablo's phone with its map of the area. Before they reached the gates of Bradley's house, Ellison pulled onto a side road that had once run off to someone's ranch and now led to a housing development.

Bradley's estate had escaped the fire, but many of the houses in the development had not. New buildings were going up again, workers in large pickups and work trucks swarming the neighborhood.

Good camouflage, Ellison said, parking at the end of the line of work trucks. He slid out of the driver's seat, and Ronan, Tiger, and Broderick crawled out from where they'd been lying low under a tarp in the back.

"Goddess," Broderick snarled as he shook himself out. "I smell like bear and ... whatever *he* is." He gave Tiger a dark look. "I said I'd help, but don't put me with the crazy again."

Tiger growled at him, but Maria swore there was humor behind it.

"Fine by me," Ellison said to Broderick. "You can scout to the north with Ronan. Tiger and I will cover the south. Take out guards, but *quietly*. Ronan, you'll teach Broderick how to do that, right?"

Ronan grinned, and Broderick made a noise of disgust. "Like I can't be more stealthy than a giant bear," Broderick muttered.

"Take out the guards, make your way to the house, and we'll disable the alarm system." Ellison studied a piece of paper before tucking it into his pocket. Pablo's girlfriend had given them instructions about how to go about bypassing the alarm without triggering it.

More trust on Ellison's part. Pablo could have instructed her to give Ellison bad guidance so he'd trip the alarm instead. Bradley might then reward Pablo. The Shifters were gambling on Pablo being more afraid of them than of Bradley.

Ellison didn't say what they'd do after they got inside. Maria knew, though. They'd corner Bradley, find out where the cubs were, then kill him.

Ellison slid back into the truck. Maria looked at him in surprise, then let out a breath when he enfolded her in his arms. He didn't squeeze, he didn't kiss her. Ellison just held her, his embrace strong.

He'd never let her fall, the hug said. Never let her falter, never let anything hurt her. Maria had been drifting, rudderless, and now, Ellison was her anchor.

He kissed Maria's cheek then her lips, his warm. "Goddess go with you," he said, his voice low. "I'll be back as soon as I can." He transferred his gaze to Pablo, and the loving look turned to ice. "You take care of her. If Maria's hurt in any way, or scared, or pissed off ... You won't live to regret it."

"I know how to do this," Pablo said, with no sign of anger. "Wipe out Bradley for me, and life will be good. That's worth sitting a couple of hours in a pickup with a nice young woman."

Ellison growled. With his arms still around Maria, feeling him rumble against her was like being held by a giant, purring cat.

Ellison kissed Maria one more time, took and pocketed Pablo's cell phone, and exited the truck. Tiger waited for him with his usual stoic patience, his assessing eyes taking in everything.

Broderick and Ronan walked up the street one way, and Tiger departed with Ellison the other.

Maria turned around to watch Ellison go. His backside in the tight jeans swayed in a fine way as he walked, sun gleaming on his hatless hair. He'd left the cowboy hat in the car, but his boots clicked on the asphalt.

Ellison didn't turn back, but Maria felt a tether between her and him, a line connecting them. She was with him, and he with her.

Pablo pulled a magazine out of his pocket, leaned back, stuck his elbow out the open window, and proceeded to read. Maria glanced over and saw that it was a home decorating magazine, open to a page on makeover ideas.

"Francesca's redoing the kitchen," Pablo said without embarrassment. "She wants me to find cabinets I like."

"I've never had a new kitchen," Maria said, before she thought about it.

"No?" Pablo shrugged. "Well, that's why I do what I do, sweetie. So I can live a little better than my parents did, which was in the gutter."

"You're a smart man. You could make a lot of money perfectly legally."

"Most of my business *is* legal. I even pay taxes on it. But I was stupid when I was younger and did some time. Prison gave me the opportunity to think about how I wanted my life to go, but prison closes a lot of doors for you."

"So does being Shifter."

Pablo lowered his magazine. "Don't let them fool you. Those Shifters might wear Collars and be bound by rules, but I'm here to tell you, they do anything they want."

"So I've seen."

Maria turned around to look after Ellison again and found him gone. He and Tiger had vanished. Though open country rolled from behind the one street of houses, she saw no sign of anyone moving through the tall grasses.

Maria had promised herself she wouldn't worry, but that was a silly promise. Of course she'd worry. Ellison was walking into a well-defended fort, with nothing but his teeth and claws and Pablo's phone—though she felt a little better that he was with Tiger.

But if anything happened to any of the Shifters, she'd have to face Liam and Dylan and tell them. Explain why she hadn't helped, why Pablo hadn't.

They'd blame Pablo for not keeping them safe, and they might punish him. From the way Pablo's fingers shook the slightest bit when he turned the pages of the magazine, he knew it too.

"What can we do?" she asked him.

Pablo didn't look up. "Stay out of it."

"Sit here until we know whether they made it or not?" Maria let out her breath. "I should at least call Andrea or Rebecca and tell them what's going on."

"And risk your call being picked up by someone in Bradley's house? I imagine he keeps his ears open for any threat."

"Can someone do that? Listen in on a cell phone call?"

"Yep. It's nothing but a signal going out through the air. If a signal's there, you better bet someone has a gadget that can pick it up. My girlfriend can do it. I bet Bradley has a guy on his permanent staff who does nothing but scan phone calls. The guy's paranoid."

Maria's heart squeezed. "Then why do you think Ellison can get inside Bradley's house without a problem?"

"I don't. But I wasn't given a choice in helping, was I? Besides, if anyone can do it, it's four stealthy, stubborn, scary-ass Shifters. I bet they get the job done with minimum casualties."

"I don't want *any* casualties."

"Not always possible. If you go after something danger-ous, there's always a risk. The bigger the prize, the bigger the risk. You have to decide whether it's worth it."

Worth risking her life to stop men like Bradley stealing children, selling them to people with money who cared nothing for anyone but themselves? It was. After Ellison stopped Bradley, Maria would make it her life's mission to find all the Shifter cubs who had been taken and release them. A good goal, better than her dream of going to school. She could always go to school when the cubs were safe.

"Whoa." Pablo dropped his magazine, staring at something in the side-view mirror. "Start the truck. Get us out of here. But slowly. Don't attract attention."

"What? Why?" Maria looked back, her heart in her throat, even as she slid behind the wheel. "Oh … "

She saw it now too. A long black limousine, slowly sliding its way up the narrow, dirty street, heading for the unfinished houses. Some of the builders saw it too and glanced up, curious.

Maria started the truck. She put it in gear and drove cautiously forward, her palms sweating. She'd have to go to the end of the cul-de-sac and turn around, no other way out.

The limo crept forward, not speeding up, just driving as though the person inside was looking over the houses being rebuilt. Bradley probably owned them, or maybe this wasn't Bradley at all. In any case, with luck Ellison's dusty truck would look like it belonged to one of the workers, with its owner heading out to find some late lunch or maybe more supplies.

Pablo was fidgeting with impatience, but Maria drove slowly, casually. She made the turn at the cul-de-sac, the tires crackling on loose gravel on the asphalt, and rolled back the way she'd come.

Pablo kept his face bent to the magazine, though he watched from the corner of his eye. The limo came on at its same crawl.

As Maria reached the spot where she'd started, the limo glided smoothly forward, turned its long body, and blocked the road.

Maria slammed on the brakes. Pablo's magazine fell. "Gun it. Get around them."

Maria started to, but she made herself stop. If she hurtled

the truck up through a yard and around the limo, they'd chase her, stop her, maybe shoot her and Pablo both. Besides, she had a better idea.

"No," Maria said.

"Shit, woman. That's Bradley."

"I guessed that. Wonder what he's doing here, and not holed up in his house?"

"I don't care. Aw, damn it."

Four men exited the limo. They wore casual clothes, jeans and polo shirts, no business suits in sight. They looked like businessmen out looking at their properties, except that three of the men surrounded the fourth as though they were his bodyguards. All four wore guns in holsters on their belts, no hiding them.

The fourth man was shorter and slimmer of build than the others, had a thick shock of salt-and-pepper hair, and wore wire-rimmed glasses. He looked innocuous, a man with enough money and confidence that he felt no need to dress to impress, until he turned his head and looked at Maria.

The cold in his eyes made her gasp. At five paces away, the chill of him seeped over her, a man with no remorse, no conscience. He could tell his three bodyguards to open fire on the truck, killing her and Pablo without a word, even in front of the construction workers, and walk away without worry.

Pablo's hand went down his jeans to his ankle holster, but Maria put her hand on his arm. "Wait."

"I can get off at least two shots before they can."

"*Wait.*"

Pablo started muttering in Spanish, asking Mary, the

mother of God, to protect him from crazy bitches who thought they were invincible because they ran with Shifters.

Maria ignored him, opened the door of the truck, and hopped out. She spread her hands and kept them out to her sides so they'd see she had no weapons.

Even so, two of the bodyguards drew pistols, holding them close by their sides, but definitely training them on her.

"Mr. Bradley?" Maria asked, as though the guns didn't make her nervous. "I'm Maria. I was hoping I could speak with you."

CHAPTER FOURTEEN

W ere you?" Bradley's voice was flat, uninflected. "I don't know you. I know Mr. Marquez there, but not you."

"You know *about* me. I work for the Shifters—well, they make me work for them. Your men have followed me when I'm out with their cubs. I know you took one of them today. I asked Mr. Marquez to bring me to your house so I could tell you I can get you more Shifter cubs if you want them. If you'll pay me, that is. They use me as a babysitter a lot, so I'm left alone with them all the time."

Bradley's gaze remained on Maria while she spoke, then he flicked it to the truck. "If that's true, why are you here and not at my front gate?"

"I was trying to talk Mr. Marquez into it." Maria smiled. "He's afraid of you, you see. He brought me this far, but refused to tell me where to go from here. When he saw you, he wanted us to run away, but I *really* want to talk to you. I need the money, and here's an opportunity."

Bradley assessed Maria without changing expression. Good thing he wasn't Shifter, because he'd scent the deception pouring off her. If she could keep him interested, while Ellison and the others got into his house, he'd have a nice surprise waiting when he went home.

"I'm willing to hear your suggestions," Bradley said. He gestured to the limo. "Ride with me, and be my guest."

Maria didn't need Pablo to tell her not to get into that car. "Can't we talk here?" *Out in the open, with witnesses.*

"No. There's nothing to be afraid of, Ms. ... "

"Ortega." No sense in lying. He could check.

"Ms. Ortega. We'll talk, we'll have coffee, and you'll go. But only if Mr. Marquez comes with us."

"Of course," Maria said. "He's good at business. He's advising me."

"I see."

Bradley didn't move, but the two bodyguards who'd taken out their pistols went to the truck. One aimed his gun through the door Maria had left open, the other went around. Pablo slid out his side of the truck, and let the goon pat him down and take his weapon.

Pablo's face was a careful blank, but his eyes held molten fury. Bradley waited until Pablo was in the limo, then he ushered Maria ahead of him as he walked to the limo's open door. The bodyguard who'd taken Pablo's gun got into the pickup and started it with the keys Maria had left, waiting to follow.

Maria swallowed her misgivings, climbed inside the leather-seated limo, and sank down next to Pablo. She tried not to flinch when the door slammed shut, enclosing them in a cushy, cigar-scented, dark-windowed prison.

Bradley had four bodyguards surrounding his house today, Ellison noted after he and Tiger had sniffed around then met up with Broderick and Ronan. Four guards, four Shifters. Poor bastards didn't stand a chance.

Ellison was about to give the order to take down the guards when he saw Bradley's limo leave from the semicircle of the drive and roll down the lane to the gate.

"Damn it."

The man hadn't seen them coming—couldn't have. The other guards remained in place, not on alert, not altering their pace. Bradley could be heading down to the nearest convenience store for beer and cigarettes for all Ellison knew.

The limousine turned in the direction of Austin, which meant in the direction of the housing development a couple miles away. No reason Bradley should enter the development, but just in case ...

"Tiger, run back to Maria and tell her Bradley's out, and to be careful. We'll get inside and wait for him."

"What if he's gone all day?" Broderick asked.

Ronan answered. "Then we wait all day. We'll give him a little welcome-home party." He grinned, his eyes flashing the red of an enraged bear.

Tiger said nothing. He acknowledged Ellison's order by turning around and fading back into the grasses. In a second or two, Ellison could no longer see him.

He'd sent Tiger, because the man was faster than any Shifter he knew, and the guards would never spot him. Tiger would be there and back in five minutes, and not even breathe hard.

"Let's go," Ellison said.

"Now it's three against four," Broderick said. "Four with automatic weapons."

"Four against three Shifters with built-in weapons," Ronan said, never losing his feral smile. He brought up his hand and curled it like claws. "They won't know what hit them."

"We should wait for the crazy," Broderick said, jerking his chin the direction Tiger had disappeared.

"No, because I want this quiet, with limited bloodshed," Ellison countered. He'd save the bloodiness for Bradley. "We don't need every cop in the county bearing down on us when someone reports Shifters rampaging at the big house. I want to get Bradley first."

Broderick let out a breath. "I see your point. Fine. We'll hit them fast and hard, knock them out, take their weapons. If we're quiet enough, the fourth one won't realize what's happened until too late."

Ellison gave him a nod. "You got it. Ready?"

"More than ready," Ronan growled. "They'll see what happens when they try to take my cub."

"Try not to kill anyone," Ellison said.

"Me?" Ronan touched his chest, brown eyes going wide. "I'm a big teddy bear. With a Collar that keeps me tame. I wouldn't hurt a fly."

"I know." Ellison grinned at him. "I've seen you catch them in your house and release them outside. Just put these guys down, and we'll go from there."

Without further word, the three separated, slinking

through the tall grasses toward the house. More bluebonnets, Ellison noted as they went. The Texas state flower, its lupine-like stalks thrusting up toward the sunlight, made the meadow almost shimmer blue. The blossoms weren't as thick here as they'd been on the banks of the pond, but they were still plentiful.

Maria was like these flowers, which could lie dormant for long stretches of time, then burst out with amazing, passionate color. Ellison's thoughts flashed to Maria clinging to him in the pond, her legs wrapping him, the feeling of being inside her, watching the water bead on her skin as her head went back in pleasure.

Once they finished with Bradley, Ellison was carrying her to his bed. Period. They'd talk about mate-claims, and forever, later—after he satisfied himself and her with a long night of sweet, hot lovemaking. Ellison would have to go slow with her, he knew that. Slow goodness would be a fine thing.

The guard on his side of the house passed two steps away, never seeing Ellison crouching in the grass. Ellison rose silently behind him, letting his hands change to his Shifter-beast's. Those hands went around the guard's neck, one jerk cutting off his air, rendering him unconscious.

Ellison lowered the man to the ground, plucked up the frightening-looking automatic sidearm, and hoped he could figure out if the thing had a safety.

He never heard a footstep, but suddenly Tiger was beside him, appearing in the grasses where Ellison had stood only a moment before.

"He has Maria," Tiger said.

Ellison had opened his mouth to swear, but he sucked in a breath. "What? You mean Bradley?"

"He took her inside the long car and drove her to the house."

Ellison's entire body went cold. He'd never been so cold. Numbness spread from his heart down his spine, paralyzing him.

He has Maria.

"Pablo was supposed to protect her," he said, lips stiff.

Tiger didn't answer. He never did when he knew it was useless. At least he didn't offer any meaningless platitudes.

"He's a dead man." Ellison said. He started forward, ready to stride down the little slope to the house, but Tiger put a hand on his arm.

Ellison registered that Tiger rarely offered his touch, so this was unusual, but the thought was dim. Ellison's body was tight, the feral in him ready to kill.

"Your plan is good," Tiger said. "We stay with your plan."

Ellison struggled to breathe. At that moment, he couldn't remember what the damn plan was. *Bradley had his mate.*

No, Tiger was right. Sneak up on the house, disable the alarm, slip inside, find Bradley, and choke off his empire at the source. They had the guards' guns. No one needed to know that Shifters had been here at all.

Ellison nodded. "Yes," he managed to say. "We stay with the plan."

Tiger released him. He led the way, moving in silence for such a big man, down the slope to rendezvous with Ronan and Broderick.

"That asshole's history," Broderick said when Ellison whispered the news. "No one messes with our females."

For once, Ellison agreed with him. When they played

out the Challenge, Ellison would pound Broderick, but right now, Broderick wanted Maria out of there as much as he did.

Ronan had subdued the fourth guard, and he handed Tiger the holstered automatic weapon he'd retrieved. Tiger looked over the gun, and then silently handed it back. Ronan gave him a *whatever* look and buckled the second weapon over his shoulder.

Ellison took the radio from the guard he'd knocked out and the second one Ronan had and tucked both in his belt. He then searched his guy for a cell phone, switched it off, and threw it as hard as he could into the meadow.

"Here comes the car," Broderick said.

They hid, the four peering through brush around the house, animals watching their prey. The black limo pulled to a stop in the semicircular drive, and Ellison's pickup stopped behind it. The back door of the limo opened. Bodyguards emerged first, then a quiet-looking Pablo.

Maria's shapely leg in jeans came out, followed by the rest of her, her white cotton blouse tugged by the breeze. She waited, looking unworried, for the next man, a smaller guy in glasses with graying hair.

The feral in Ellison rose up again. He knew, from the way the others treated him, that this was Bradley. His enemy. His prey. His kill.

The first bodyguard went into the house through the front door, the second signaling Pablo to follow. Pablo stopped, saying something, and the bodyguard pointed a gun at him.

Maria turned around, planting her feet, and started talking to Bradley. And talking and talking. She gesticulated toward Pablo and back to the limo, but she didn't look afraid.

"What's she doing?" Ronan whispered.

"Giving us a window," Ellison said. Goddess bless her. "The bodyguard's turned off the alarm. Let's get inside before it's on again."

———

"Pablo's the only one who's ever wanted to help me," Maria said to Bradley as they stood on the wide brick doorstep. The door to Bradley's vast house lay open behind her, the bodyguard who'd opened it waiting impatiently inside it.

"So why don't you leave the Shifters and work for him?" Bradley asked. He sounded mildly curious, not annoyed.

"Because he's a criminal, and you can imagine what he wants women who work for him to do. I must get away from the Shifters, but not with him. I need money to do that. That's why I'm here."

Bradley watched her, again with little change in expression. Pablo had been right to say the man had no emotions.

"Let's go inside, Ms. Ortega. My bodyguards get anxious if I'm out in the open too much. Mr. Marquez will be given something to drink in the living room, while we talk in my office."

Pablo raised his hands, conceding, and walked inside. He'd balked at the doorway, pretending to be too scared to enter, and Maria had taken the cue. If she talked enough, and the door was open long enough, Ellison, if he'd gotten into position, would be able to slip inside. If not ... well, she was back to hoping Pablo's girlfriend had given them the right codes.

She walked into the house, Bradley came behind her, and the last bodyguard shut the door. The interior was vast, the foyer rising two floors straight up, with a wrought-iron railed balcony encircling the second level. Doors opened out from this balcony, which flowed in a circle around the twisting staircase.

The first and second bodyguards peeled Pablo off to a room beneath the balcony, while the third and fourth body-guard led Maria upstairs following Bradley. Bradley ushered Maria into a room that faced the rear of the house, its window overlooking a meadow studded with bluebonnets, which were bursting into full spring ecstasy.

Bradley motioned for Maria to sit in front of a long empty desk, and went to a wet bar, where he poured cold bottled water into a glass with ice and brought the bottle and glass to her. The bodyguards took up positions on either side of the doorway.

"All right," Bradley said, resting one hip on his desk. He looked almost congenial, except for the chill nothingness in his eyes. "You say you want to help me obtain Shifter cubs for my clients. How would you do it?"

"They make me watch the brats," Maria said, wincing inwardly at the word, but telling herself to play it out. "I could bring one or two to a location where you could easily pick them up. If I had known you were coming when I was with Olaf yesterday, I would have kept the other Shifters away."

"Hmm," Bradley said. "You could get away with that once, maybe. What happens when the next set of cubs you're supposed to be watching also get taken? They'll be suspi-cious, don't you think?" His tone held faint scorn.

He didn't believe her. Maria shut her eyes, bunched her fists, and tried to look helpless and desperate. "If you pay me enough, I only need to do it once or twice. Then I can take the money and leave town—leave the country. I can guarantee three, maybe four cubs. The Shifter families don't have that many kids, so you won't get much more than that anyway."

Her heart burned. If those precious cubs were lost, the entire community would be devastated.

"Might work," Bradley conceded. "You'd have to make sure the cubs weren't anywhere near any of the adults."

"I could. They watch me pretty carefully, but they also consider me only a servant."

"They'll punish you if the cubs you're looking after go missing."

"They will." Maria drew a breath and took on a resigned expression. "But they won't kill me. I'd be ready to go after the second drop."

"And you want—what? Maybe ten grand a cub?"

Ten grand. If Bradley was willing to pay her that much to lure cubs away, how much more must his clients be paying to receive them? She felt sick.

"I think that will work." Now to have him let her and Pablo out of the house so Ellison could continue with his plan. She rose. "Adios, Mr. Bradley. I'd better have Pablo drive me back, before the Shifters punish me for staying away too long. It's my one day off a month."

"You can go, certainly." Bradley's mouth turned up at the corners. "But I'll have Mr. Marquez stay a while as my guest. You give me the first cubs tomorrow, and I'll let him go home then."

Maria contrived to look worried, then she gave him a nervous smile. "He won't like that. But all right. I'll do it. I can ... "

Shouts cut off her words. The bodyguards came alert and hurried out the door, and Bradley's half smile vanished.

The cold he'd exhibited before was nothing to the iceberg he became. All humanity left his eyes, and he came off the desk, walked back to the wet bar, and calmly took out a pistol.

Maria's heart stopped, certain he was about to shoot her dead.

"Get under the desk," he said in clipped tones, then walked past her out of the room.

Maria heard the unmistakable snarl of a wolf, then the roar of a bear and the uncanny, breathy growl of a tiger. Then shots firing, the chug, chug, chug of a semiautomatic.

Her heart pounded in fear. But the animal snarls only escalated, and one of the bodyguards cried out. Maria raced out of the room.

Below the balcony, two wolves fought to tear a gun out of one bodyguard's hands. Ronan rose to his full Kodiak bear height, bringing his paw down on a second bodyguard. He didn't even have to use his claws.

The man collapsed, and then a puddle of blood spread out from under him. Ronan blinked his bear eyes at him in surprise, then at Pablo, who stepped out from the living room, a large gun in his hand.

A giant Bengal tiger was flowing up the stairs. One of the bodyguards at the top, face paling, shot him. Once, twice.

Tiger came on. The man stepped back. "Mother fu—"

Then Tiger was on him. The weapon flew wide. The

remaining bodyguard brought his gun around to shoot Tiger again, but Maria sprang into him from behind.

She wasn't big enough to take the man down, but he at least misfired. The bullets sprayed into the ceiling, bits of plaster and dust raining down on them.

Tiger opened his mouth, his teeth gigantic, spittle running down them, as he turned to the remaining body-guard. The light in his yellow eyes wasn't sane.

"Tiger!" Maria yelled. "No!"

Tiger jerked his head up, caught by her voice, but the rage didn't leave his eyes. He snarled once again, but Ellison was there, leaping into him, knocking him away from the man.

Tiger roared in fury, but Ellison growled, and Tiger finally loped away back down the stairs.

Ellison turned to the bodyguard. Ellison's wolf was huge, his hair up along his neck, his ears flat with his red-eyed snarling. The bodyguard dropped his weapon and fell to his knees.

"Please. I got a wife. I got kids," the man said. "I just work here because it pays good."

Ellison stopped his charge an inch from the guy's face, jaws snapping in irritation. Maria reached down and picked up the gun. It was heavy, and she didn't know how to hold it. The danger locked in the firm piece of metal scared her, but she figured it was better she had it than the bodyguard.

"Go home," she said to him. "Hurry. Where's Bradley?"

A second wolf and Ronan came up the stairs, the stair-case creaking under the Kodiak's weight. Bradley was nowhere in sight.

"He hasn't come past me," Pablo called from below.

"He has a panic room," the bodyguard said, still on his knees. "Through that door and at the end of the hall." He pointed. "Sealed tight. He holes up there when things get bad."

"Thank you," Maria said. "Go now."

The bodyguard hauled himself to his feet. His face was gray, eyes filled with fear. "Thanks. Thanks." He stuttered the words then turned to go past Ellison, Broderick, and finally Ronan.

Ronan couldn't resist giving a little growl and swatting at him. The former bodyguard hurtled down the stairs, ran past Pablo, who only watched him without interest, and sprinted out of the house.

Maria opened the door the bodyguard had indicated, then felt teeth on her wrist. Ellison had his mouth, ever so gently, on her arm, looking at her with admonishment. *Stay here,* he was saying. Maria sighed and stepped back to let the Shifters go through first.

The hall ended in another innocuous door, but it hung partway open, revealing a steel door behind it. The second door had no handle, only a keypad.

Maria reasoned that a man like Bradley would have been too cautious to use the same code for his panic room as his front door. But the combined might of two Shifter wolves and a Kodiak bear was soon breaking the seal on the door. Tiger stood back, growling under his breath, tail swishing the slightest bit over the hall carpet.

"Tiger, what's wrong?" Maria asked.

Ellison glanced up. Tiger's warning rumble escalated, and then he roared.

Ellison, Ronan, and Broderick sprang away from the

door as it gave, the wolves diving flat as Tiger did. Ronan, too big to do anything but back up, knocked over a delicate gilded side table, the trinkets on its top shattering.

The steel door burst open, and two large, sleek wildcats hurtled out, straight into the wolves and Ronan.

Maria screamed. Tiger rose, but instead of rushing to aid the others, he ran at Maria, herding her back onto the foyer's balcony. Once she was there, he turned and sprinted back down the hall.

What was Bradley doing with *Shifters?*

Her chest constricted. Oh, mother of God. *What happens to the cubs when they get too big to handle?* she'd asked Pablo.

The cheetahs had been wearing Collars, so not feral. Stolen, she guessed, from a Shifter family somewhere. How long ago? Had the clients given them back to Bradley once they tired of them? Had they been here all this time? Prisoners? How many more did he have?

The hallway was a confusion of fur and snarling, yelps and roars. She saw Ellison fall, cheetah claws raking across his fur. He was up in a second, wolf maw closing over the cheetah's neck. He could break it in the next moment.

"Ellison!" she shouted. "Ellison, they're cubs!"

CHAPTER FIFTEEN

Ellison showed no sign of hearing, but the second cheetah, squirming away from Ronan, knocked into him. Tiger was roaring, but not fighting. Maybe he understood. Tiger was always so protective of the cubs.

Maria had seen Scott crazed from his Transition, striking out before Ronan or Rebecca could stop him. If these two were going through the same thing ...

They'd stop at nothing to fight their perceived enemies, their killing instinct wound high.

Bradley must be behind them, in that room. Or was he? Would he have run into a room from which there was no escape?

Maria looked swiftly around, taking in the layout of the hallway relative to the rest of the house. She turned and hurried down the stairs and looked out the front door, the gun awkward in her hands, but she feared discarding it. The other guards were subdued, not dead.

Ellison's pickup remained in the driveway, but the limo

was gone. Had the driver fled? Or had he driven around to pick up Bradley, who could have escaped out the back? Maria moved through the house again, looking around for another way out—faster than trying to run around the vast building and encounter who knew how many walls or other obstacles.

In the rear of the ground floor, Maria found a kitchen, a huge, elegant room with stainless steel appliances and warm wooden cabinetry. Maybe she should show it to Pablo, and have him take photos for his girlfriend.

A door from this led out to a wide area between the house and five-car garage, a building that looked as though it had once been a stables. An iron stairwell snaked down the house next to the kitchen, a fire escape. High above was an ornate door, closed, that led back into the house.

Bradley wasn't on the fire escape. He was running across the yard toward the garage. The limo raced up from the other side of the house, dust flying as the driver headed to help Bradley.

Maria raised the gun. It was not very big, but square, like a machine gun with a very short barrel. She aimed down at the limo's tires and squeezed the trigger.

Three bullets spurted from the weapon, and the kick nearly knocked her off her feet. The shots came nowhere near the tires—they popped into the ground by the limo driver's door and open window.

The limo stopped, the driver staring at Maria with fear on his face. She lifted the gun again, her hands shaking.

The limo jumped forward, swung around, and raised dust roaring off the other way. Bradley glared after it, then at Maria, and ducked inside the garage.

"Ellison!" Maria yelled. "Ronan! Bradley's out here!"

Her shouts brought no one. The man was going to go for whatever car was in there and get away.

Maria aimed the gun again and fired a few shots to ping against the ground in front of the garage doors. The weapon's metal felt hot in her hands, and the gun's kick, though she was ready for it this time, still made her take a few steps backward.

All was silent within the garage. Maybe fear of a young woman with a gun she obviously couldn't control would keep Bradley in place for a moment.

Maria risked it. She ran back into the house, through the kitchen and out to the staircase hall. The fight had moved to the balcony above, the wolves and cheetahs rolling in a free-for-all, Ronan having backed off as though waiting to find a good opening. Tiger crouched on the stairs, growling, unhappy.

And where had Pablo disappeared to? The man was nowhere in sight, though Ellison's truck was still in front. Pablo hadn't taken it, made good his escape, and stranded them there. But where was he?

The iron railing above her creaked and strained. As Maria looked up, one of the supports snapped. The railing teetered under the weight of the fighting animals, then came down. With it tumbled the wolves and cheetahs—one wolf, Broderick, scrabbling to keep his hold on the balcony until the last minute.

Maria fled out of the way. Ellison hit the stairs on his back, the cheetahs' limbs flailing until they landed on him, claws raking as they struggled to gain their feet. Ellison, still wolf, rolled out from under them, coming to a stand on four paws, panting hard.

Broderick managed to crawl back up to the upper floor, shifting to his half beast to do it. He morphed to fully human as he stood up, trying to catch his breath.

Tiger moved. He came down the stairs almost on his belly, heading for the cheetahs, his ears back, teeth bared. The cheetahs looked at him in uncertainty, then the mad look came back into their eyes, and they charged him, Collars sparking.

At the same time, men poured into the house from the front, the back, all armed. Bradley or one of his guards must have called for backup. A man like Bradley could afford the best, and the men who came in, at least two dozen of them, were large, grim-faced, and hard-muscled—likely ex-military, ex-mercenary, ex-convict. They aimed at the Shifters, who'd be mowed down.

Maria yelled a warning. A few of the hard-eyed men glanced at her then walked on, not seeing her as a threat. She still had the gun, held down and behind her back, but her fingers were slick on the trigger. Could she shoot another human being? And if she started shooting, would they simply train weapons on her and obliterate her in seconds?

Her cry had alerted Ellison. He was moving again, racing up the stairs, Ronan coming down toward him. Tiger saw the men and roared, rising to his full height. He put himself in front of the cheetahs as the first shots were fired, a bullet bloodying his fur.

Ellison turned and leapt over the last curve of staircase, landing on one of the mercenaries before he could get off a shot. His Collar sparked as he rolled over the man, the gun clattering away.

The others split off through the staircase hall, aiming, firing. Tiger herded the cheetahs back upstairs, toward the room with the steel door. Ronan and Broderick had ducked behind walls when the bullets started flying. They were big, tough Shifters, but shots could still kill them.

Ellison fought alone. He bloodied the man, while one of the merc's colleagues tried to get a clear shot at him. The rest were moving up the stairs, or through the house, hunting, searching, shooting.

What could Maria do? Whatever happened, she had to stop Bradley. And save Ellison. As soon as Ellison came up from subduing the man he fought, the second man would shoot him.

If this were one of the many TV shows she watched, she'd come up with some clever way to bring down all the bad guys, who'd obligingly drop weapons and look defeated and disgruntled. Maria had the feeling it wouldn't be that easy in real life. These men were professionals, who would shoot Ellison and the others, get Bradley safely away, and then go have coffee.

Maria ducked into the living room, where Bradley's men had originally taken Pablo, but the room was empty. She plucked a cell phone from the man Pablo had shot in the hall and punched in a number. Bradley had called backup; she could too.

She'd dialed Dylan's phone, but she wanted to cry when Connor answered. "You're all right!" she whispered.

"Yeah. Groggy, but all right. Where are you?"

"Where's Dylan?"

"Driving. Maria, I asked you—where are you?"

"At Bradley's. We need help."

Connor started to speak again, but his words cut off to be replaced by Liam's voice. "Lass, you stay put. Make sure Bradley stays put. We're coming. Where to, exactly?"

Maria opened her mouth to answer, then the cell phone was yanked from her hand, and a punch landed across her face. She went down, pain exploding through her, the gun falling from her numb fingers.

Ellison was there in the next moment, the giant gray wolf slamming into the man who'd hit Maria. The merc lost hold of his weapon, sending it sliding across the rug. Ellison landed on him, breaking the arm the man stretched toward the gun. The merc screamed, and then again as Ellison's paws rendered his head a bloody mess.

Another weapon clicked, a second merc with an automatic weapon raised and pointed at Ellison. Maria scrambled to her feet, face aching from the first punch. She launched herself at the man, thinking to grab his arm to train the gun away from Ellison.

Crimson burst over the merc's face, and he fell gurgling. Dead. Maria gaped past him to see Pablo, his small pistol back in his hands, his eyes almost as cold as Bradley's. The bang of the gun filled the room and made Maria's ears ring.

Ellison climbed off the other man he'd knocked down, that merc out. Ellison's wolf sides heaved, his jaw bloody, scratches and blood in his fur. He shook himself, nose wrinkling at the smell of death.

"You're welcome," Pablo said to them. "Where's Bradley? I can't afford to let him live."

"In the garage." Maria's jaw hurt when she spoke, and she worked it. "Last I saw. He could be long gone by now."

"Let's go find out." Pablo had lowered his gun but didn't holster it. "I called my own backup, but if we don't get the hydra, I'm a dead man."

Ellison shifted. He rose onto strong legs, his torso bruised and abraded, his face bloody. He limped to Maria, still breathing hard, and put an arm around her.

"You all right, sweetheart? I'm sorry—I couldn't stop him in time."

Maria rubbed her cheek. "I will be. I've had worse."

She had, when she'd been prisoner of the feral Shifters, but the answer made Ellison's eyes fill with fury. His arm tightened around her, but his touch on her face was tenderness itself.

"They found Connor," Maria said quickly. "I told Liam to come, but I didn't get a chance to tell him where." The cell phone on the floor was cracked and dark.

"My girlfriend will tell him," Pablo said. "She's hacked all the calls in and out of here. From a safe distance—I told her to get the hell out of town until this is over." He gave Ellison an admonishing look, as though Ellison should have done the same with Maria. Not that Maria would have listened.

Pablo led the way out, through another door and around to a back hall. More gunfire sounded, and over it came the roars of Tiger and Ronan. Maria wanted to run and make sure they were all right, but Ellison steered her firmly out.

They had to fight in the kitchen. Ellison shoved Maria down behind a counter and shifted into the state between wolf and human as more of Bradley's mercs opened fire on them. A few of Pablo's men—one of them Maria recognized as a mechanic at Pablo's car shop—were pinned down here, firing back. Pablo joined them, Ellison slinking under their fire to tackle one of Bradley's mercs.

Maria crawled behind the counter to the door, then sprinted out. Another two mercs were down outside, one unmoving, one groaning, both unarmed. Maria hurried past them in time to see one of the garage doors open, a gray Cadillac emerging.

She'd dropped her weapon when the other man had knocked her down, and Pablo had grabbed it on the way out, giving it to one of his men in the kitchen who'd run out of ammo. Now Maria could only stand helplessly and watch the car come out of the garage. Bradley was getting away, but what could she do?

The answer came from a deafening roar behind her. The sound pounded through the house, vibrating it like a small earthquake.

Maria had heard it once before, a lion's roar. The lion Shifter that bounded toward the car was Dylan, black maned, his Collar silent, rage in his white blue eyes. He roared again, an alpha male in his full strength. Behind him came Spike, his naked human form covered with tatts, and another black-maned lion—Sean. Sean was followed by a wolf that looked like Ellison, only a little smaller and finer boned.

The wolf stopped beside Maria, then it froze as the Cadillac accelerated, swerving to avoid the Shifters. Maria saw Bradley behind the wheel, his face still expressionless, his glasses shining.

Beside Maria, the wolf's shape distorted and jerked, a

Shifter changing before it wanted to. It rose into the form of Deni, who stared at the car, her face set in horror.

"That's the one," Deni said, her voice barely a whisper. "That's the car that hit me."

Ellison, in his wolf form now, along with Pablo, had run up to Maria's side in time to hear her. Ellison looked at Deni, understanding and rage in his wolf's eyes.

He burst away and charged the the car, slamming into its side and forcing it to turn. Sean ran and leapt, landing on the car's trunk, and Dylan planted himself in front of it, his lion's roar breaking the air.

Bradley jerked the car sideways, tires sliding, choking dust rising high. His hand spun the wheel until the car came out of its skid, and he headed straight for Maria and Deni.

Ellison and Dylan tried to sprint ahead of it, Sean climbing to the roof, his claws leaving long gouges in the car's body.

Deni, motionless, watched the Cadillac come at her. Pablo grabbed both women to yank them out of the way, but Deni came alive.

She snatched the gun out of Pablo's hands, aimed it, and fired three practiced shots through the windshield and into Bradley's head.

The car kept coming. Maria slammed herself into Deni and Pablo, pushing them out of the way. The car rushed past them, Bradley's dead foot still on the gas, and crashed, head-on, into the house.

The car's engine spluttered and died, and all was silent.

CHAPTER SIXTEEN

Ellison stood in the ring at the fight club, naked, flexing his hands, ready to go. His ribs hurt, his torso was streaked with deep scratches, and his neck ached from too many shocks of his Collar, but still he was here.

Shifters filled the vast space of the abandoned hay barn out east of Austin, the darkness broken by trashcan fires, huge flashlights, and LED lanterns. Broderick climbed over the cinder blocks that marked out the ring, a big smile on his face. He had come away from the fight at Bradley's relatively unscathed and exuded confidence he'd win the Challenge.

Fuck that.

Ellison felt the pull of the growing mate bond with Maria, stretching between him and her as she stood outside the ring with Spike and Ronan, Ellison's seconds.

Connor stood next to them, too keyed up to stay home. He'd been restless and hungry after they'd all made it back to Shiftertown, Connor eating everything in sight and insisting he go to the fight club. Cubs weren't technically allowed at the fight club, but Connor was given slack tonight, with the approval of all Shifters.

Though he wouldn't fight, Ellison imagined that Connor would find a way to work off his steam. Apparently Bradley had taken him because a woman had asked Bradley to find her a strapping young Shifter for her entertainment. Pablo had related this after he and his girlfriend, restored to Austin, had gone through Bradley's desk and computer.

Maria stood close to Connor, her shoulder touching his. Ellison scented her goodness, her courage and passion.

He also scented that she was very, very angry.

Maria had argued long and hard for Ellison to not meet Broderick tonight. By the time they'd all limped back to Shiftertown, Maria driving, Ellison was sore, tired, clawed all over, and aching from a couple bullets that had grazed his arm.

At the same time, he was buoyant. Maria loved him. The mate bond was forming. He'd had the joy of holding her in his arms, being inside her yesterday in the soothing pond.

Tonight, after he battered Broderick until the man begged for mercy, Ellison would carry her home and take her to bed.

That is, if he could still stand up.

Around them, Shifters shouted and laughed. Broderick's pack stood behind him to cheer him on. The air was thick with scents of anticipation, eagerness, and mating frenzy. A Challenge brought out the mating need in Shifters, both male and female.

Pablo had come, betting on the fight in his quiet way. Ellison guessed he'd bet on Broderick. But then, Broderick hadn't fallen from a balcony onto stairs and had two crazed cheetahs in their Transition land on him.

Dylan and Tiger had taken charge of the cheetahs. When they'd turned to human, they'd been two males in their late twenties, twins, who had lived as captives on a wealthy woman's estate in New York. The woman had asked Bradley to take them back when they hit their Transition and became too crazed.

Tiger had been solicitous of the two, and Dylan was arranging for them to be taken into the Austin Shiftertown.

They owed another debt to Pablo. He'd stayed behind after the Shifters had piled into various vehicles to leave, taking care of the remaining mercs and saying he'd make Bradley's death and the torn-up house look like a gang hit. Bradley had made many enemies.

Pablo had looked around the house and at the kitchen with approval, and said he'd try to buy the place. Ellison suspected he'd provide jobs for Bradley's mercenaries, now that their boss was dead. The battle today was all to Pablo's gain.

As for Deni ...

She stood straight and tall beside Maria. Shooting Bradley seemed to have released something in her. The haunting worry in her eyes had gone, and her cubs, standing behind her, were there to comfort her. Whether she'd thrown off the episodes of her memory blanking remained to be seen, but Deni now knew exactly what had happened to her, and who had done it.

Bradley might have been trying to capture her—maybe he'd mistaken her for a cub, or maybe someone had asked for a female Shifter the same way the woman had asked for someone Connor's age. Ellison's rage hadn't calmed down about that.

Maria had declared her new mission to track down all those who'd purchased Shifters—adult or cub—and release the captives. Ellison agreed. They'd start tomorrow.

Tonight, he needed to take out Broderick.

Two refs stood between the two combatants. They thumped their fists, one over the other, and yelled, "Fight."

The refs scattered, and Ellison went for Broderick. Broderick sidestepped, whirled, and shifted at the same time. Mistake. Broderick landed in Ellison's furred arms, Ellison rising into his half-Shifter beast.

Broderick squirmed away, lithe and strong as his wolf. Ellison followed, the pain in his ribs slowing him down, his Collar going off. Broderick took advantage to shift to his half beast and catch Ellison across the torso with his clawed hands.

Ellison danced back, landing on all fours as a wolf. He launched himself upward, latching his teeth into Broderick's throat.

He found his mouth full of the loose fur as Broderick came down wolf. He snarled and shook, flailing Ellison's body, but Ellison held on.

Broderick finally twisted all the way around, and Ellison's teeth slipped. Blood dripped from the wound in Broderick's neck, the metallic taste winding Ellison into a frenzy.

"No killing!" one of the refs yelled.

Too late. Ellison's rage was up. Broderick wanted to steal his mate. In the wild, males tried to abduct females all the time, until the formal Challenge and its rules had been set up to protect the scarce females. These days, Challenges didn't end in the kill, but Ellison wanted it.

He went for Broderick's throat again. This time, Broderick shifted into his half-wolf beast, catching Ellison, raising him high, and throwing him down.

Ellison landed in a whump of dust, the bruised ribs stabbing him, new wounds opening. His Collar was sparking too, slowing his roll to his feet.

He stood panting, trying to raise his head. Damn Broderick. He needed to go down.

Ellison backed up a few steps, but Broderick charged him. Ellison came up, and the two males met, both wolves now, snarling, biting, clawing.

Broderick chomped on the back of Ellison's neck, and Ellison rolled away, wanting to groan in pain. He scrambled to get his paws under him, the light of the fires in the abandoned hay barn starting to blur. Broderick was a blur too, the noise around him a hum of confusion.

Something brushed past him, something that smelled sweet and good, and of mate.

"Stop!" he heard Maria shout. "Stop the fight!"

Ellison blinked. The lights were still fuzzy around the edges, but he saw Maria clearly, inside the ring, between him and Broderick. The refs were coming for her, shock on their faces.

A big rule of the fight club was that no one, *no one,* stopped a fight once it started. The only stopping was when an opponent yielded, or the refs thought one of them too far gone and needed to be contained.

No one watching was allowed to touch the fighters, and

certainly not to enter the ring. Especially a human. Especially a human *female*.

The two refs, big Felines, were heading to grab Maria and drag her out. Ellison put his wolf body between her and them, growling hard.

Outside the ring, Connor said, "Maria, you can't do that."

Tiger stepped over the barrier. Ellison noticed no one tried to stop *him*. "Don't touch her," Tiger said clearly.

The refs halted. Broderick shifted into his human form and put his hands on his hips. Goddess, the man stank.

"You can't stop the Challenge," Broderick said to Maria. "Or he forfeits." He grinned at her. "You don't want that, now do you?"

"He was already hurt before he walked in," Maria said angrily. "You knew that. You should have put it off."

"Hey, he picked the time and place."

Ellison leaned back against Maria, a fine place to be, and she put her arms around his neck. "Do it some other time. You can stop this."

Ellison's body decided to shift. He didn't want to—he felt stronger as wolf—but Maria with her arms around him made him change form back to human male. He ended up with Maria's arms still around him, pulling him close.

"Hey, love," he said, his voice barely working. "You're crazy, you know that?"

"I'm taking you home," Maria said. "I don't want to see you hurting anymore."

Around them, the crowd stopped screaming and booing and moved closer to listen. Shifters could never mind their own business.

"Let me finish this first," Ellison said, the words rasping. "A mate always answers a Challenge."

"Doesn't matter. Even if Broderick wins, I'll refuse him, and come back to you anyway."

Some of Ellison's tension left him, and his breath became less labored. His ribs started to feel better too. The healing touch of the mate. He hadn't quite believed in such a power before—especially when the mate was human—but he did now.

Ellison leaned to her, his forehead against hers. "Look around you. All these males here would want you as mate. They call you fair game, but you're the one who does the choosing. Anyone you want, for the taking."

"I already chose."

Her words poured strength into Ellison's body. Enough strength for him to rise up and kick Broderick's sorry behind? Well, maybe not.

Maria was speaking again, her words flowing, but his heart only heard the peace of her voice.

"You told me I should stop surviving and start living. You should too, Ellison. Stop just getting by, and show me how to live. Live life with *me*."

Ellison felt the smile spread over his face. "Oh, sweetheart. You've done it now."

"Done what?"

"Made me know the mate bond is real. I love you, Maria."

Maria took a sharp breath, then her answering smile blossomed. "I love *you*, Ellison Rowe."

Ellison kissed her. This kiss went on ... and on.

Shifters around them cheered. Or howled, roared, whistled, or made ribald remarks. Damned nosy neighbors.

"Aw, shit." Broderick spit on the ground. "Damn it, I can't compete with this. You're a lucky dickhead, Ellison." He heaved a long and aggrieved sigh. "I withdraw the Challenge."

His family groaned. Deni whooped, and Connor followed suit. Other Shifters said, "Awww," and clapped and cheered.

"You're still an asshole," Broderick growled. But he came forward, holding out his hand.

Ellison turned and put his into it, making sure his grip was as strong as Broderick's. He kept his other arm around Maria so he wouldn't fall down.

"Come on," Broderick said. "Get yourself dressed, and I'll buy you a beer at Liam's place."

"Rain check," Ellison said, warming as he drew Maria to him again. "I'm going home."

———

Ellison carried Maria into his bedroom at the very back of the house, slamming the door with his cowboy-booted foot.

Maria had never seen his bedroom. In the light from the lamp beside his bed, she saw a large map of Texas on one wall, a red pin in the center marking Austin. The flag of Texas, with its one white and one red stripe, blue field on the left bearing the lone star, hung downward on another wall. Photos of Ellison's sister, nephews, and friends were pinned up over the desk. Ellison was laughing in any snapshot he was in, saluting with a longneck beer, or tipping his cowboy hat in an exaggerated way.

She took all this in before Ellison collapsed with her onto the bed. It was a single bed, narrow, and Maria squashed against him.

"Love." Ellison rolled onto his back, rubbed his hands through his hair, and blew out his breath. "Goddess, what a day."

"It ended well." Maria rose on her elbow and tapped the tip of his nose. "You should sleep. You need to heal."

"Not yet." His voice lost its teasing note, his playfulness dissolving. "Not yet." Ellison skimmed his hand along her side to her breast. "Do you know what went through my mind when you ran into that ring tonight, all fired up?"

"Annoyance?"

Ellison dissolved into laughter. "Man, those refs are never going to let me hear the end of it. The fight club is all about the rules." He touched her face. "No, I thought you were mighty sexy running in there, telling everyone what to do with themselves. Crazy, but sexy."

"They were going to let you fight when you were already hurt," Maria said indignantly.

"You think I couldn't take Broderick in my rundown state? You wound me."

"Don't be stupid. It should be a fair fight. You have to win with skill and strength, not arrogance." She made a face. "And no way was I going to be Broderick's mate."

"I wasn't about to let you be." Ellison ran the ball of this thumb across her lips. "Then he had to go and do the noble thing, and make all of Shiftertown soft on him. But even an asshole could see that we were meant to be together."

"Broderick was good to step back."

"Nah, he'd be embarrassed if I kicked his ass when I was already hurt." Ellison grinned. "No, you're right. I was halfway down already and Broderick came through. Makes me almost like the guy." He winced and touched his ribs where Broderick had gotten in a blow. "Almost."

"You see? You should rest. We'll talk about being mates in the morning."

"Oh, no." In one quick move, Ellison rolled his body over hers, pinning her with his warm weight. "I've been waiting all day to get my arms around you again. I was thinking about us in the pond all last night and all today, remembering the bluebonnets, the sunshine. You." He skimmed his lips, warm and satin smooth, across her mouth. "Why did you decide to start making love to me, yesterday? Not that I minded."

"I wanted to." Maria slid her hands to the small of his back, his flesh warm through his shirt. "I was worried that when you finally seduced me, I would be afraid. So I thought if I did it fast, without thinking about it, then I'd know if I would be afraid. Does that sound crazy?"

"And were you?" Ellison's voice was quiet. "Afraid?"

"No." Maria dug her hands into his back, pulling him closer. "No, I wasn't. It was ... so beautiful."

"Yeah, that's a good word for it. *Fucking amazing* is another."

"That's two words."

"Whatever."

Ellison knelt back from her and skimmed her shirt up and off over her head. Cool air touched Maria's breasts, held by her satin bra, the spring breeze from the open window soft.

Ellison reached over and switched off the lamp. In the white moonlight, he unsnapped her bra, slid it off, and tossed it aside, then took time to rest his gaze on her, taking her in.

"Trouble with pond water is it's too muddy," he said. "You can't see what you want through it."

She smiled. "I know."

"Oh, sweetheart, you can make a man hard looking at him like that, and saying that."

"I only said *I know*."

"Maybe, but it was the way you said it."

Maria started laughing. She loved this man, who made her feel good, and made her laugh, at the same time he spiraled her into wanting. She reached for his belt buckle and popped the big thing open.

"Why do you wear this?" The buckle had an oil well and *Texas* emblazoned on it.

"Because I like Texas. It's big, it's bold, it's not afraid of the world. I like to brag that I'm from the most in-your-face state in the country."

"But you're from Colorado."

Ellison grinned his big grin, then subsided. "You want to know the truth?" He traced a soft pattern on her breast, which slid fire to her heart. "When my sister and I and my nephews were rounded up to be brought here, Collared and registered like cattle, I didn't know what was going to happen to us. By the time we were dumped here, left in front of this house, which was at the time a rundown pile of crap, I'd figured out one thing. Deni and I had left behind a lot of sadness, a hole where our lives used to be. I looked around at this vast place, and I decided Texas would be our new beginning. I left behind my old life and totally embraced the new, every part of it. Got me a big pickup, a flag, a belt buckle, and an accent. The hat and boots I already had, 'cause you know, *real* cowboys come from Colorado."

Maria laughed again. "You have a big ego."

"So I fit right in. But I learned to love everything Texas, my new home, my new life. It saved me."

She nodded, understanding. "Like me trying to learn to be American, and go to school, and live with Shifters."

Ellison drew his fingers up her throat and around her chin, his touch featherlight. "We're both carving out a place for ourselves." His voice went quiet. "How about we do it together?"

Words welled up inside Maria, so many words that she couldn't make them coherent. "Yes," she said softly.

The Shifter wolf flashed into his eyes and out again. "Maria, honey, yesterday, in the water, everything was slow, sensual." He slid his touch to her breast again. "Tonight, I don't know if I can be as sweet."

Maria's heart beat faster, a point of heat curling between her thighs. "I don't want sweet."

"You sure?" Ellison's breath came faster, his body tightening. "I don't want to rush you, or scare you. But if I start, I won't be able to stop."

More excitement licked through her. "I'm sure. It's not the same." She laced her fingers through his hair at the nape of his neck. "You're Ellison. You care about me. It's different."

"I do care." Ellison's voice gentled. "I love you, Maria. I've been waiting for you for so long."

Maria had been waiting for him. She hadn't known it those long years, through the misery and the pain. But she'd realized, that day she met him, when he'd touched his hat and said, "Ma'am," that her knight in shining armor had come.

"I can't ... " Ellison said. "Goddess."

He rolled off her, coming to his feet, his eyes pale gray in the moonlight. He yanked off his belt and boots, jeans and shirt, emerging bare. Bruises and abrasions were dark across his torso, but they were healing, his Shifter metabolism working on them already.

Ellison leaned down and tugged open the button of Maria's jeans. She tried to help slide them down, but he had them off in a few swift jerks, pulling the panties after them. He left her shoes, slim sandals, on her feet, too impatient to remove them.

Ellison came back onto the bed, his warm bare body over hers, lowering himself without hurting her.

That was the last thing he did gently. He skimmed back her hair from her forehead and took her mouth in a deep, long kiss. His tongue tangled hers, the kiss hot and satisfying.

His kisses fell on her throat, her breasts, her belly, back to her breasts again. Ellison closed his mouth over one nipple, suckling, until Maria arched, the tight little pain bringing out a noise of pleasure.

More kisses, down her abdomen, one pressed to her navel, and the next between her legs. Maria felt his tongue, and she cried out. Ellison licked her there, moving his tongue around her opening, plunging inside it, her hips lifting from the mattress. Maria had never felt such a thing, had never experienced this kind of fine wildness.

Because Ellison did it for pleasure alone. The feral Shifters had cared only for *their* pleasure, and for creating cubs, and hadn't been concerned about Maria.

Ellison was taking the time to show his mate pleasure, joy, how it felt to be treasured. It was loving, caring.

The sensation also had Maria winding toward climax. White fire rippled through her, radiating from Ellison's skilled tongue all the way to her fingertips. She rocked against him, her hand furrowing his hair, pulling him closer, closer.

Ellison lifted his beautiful mouth away and slid his body up hers. He enclosed her in his arms, catching her cries of climax on his lips at the same time he slid straight into her.

Maria's eyes widened. Yesterday in the water, she easing herself onto him, she'd not had this fullness. He'd filled her, yes, but tonight she had the entire length of him, and it was powerful. Ellison spread her wide, she tight and hot, the place where they joined filled with wonderful ache.

"Ellison," she said, her voice rolling through the room. "I love you!"

"I love you, Maria." His voice was fierce, his body strong. "Mate of my heart. Together. We do this *together*."

"Always." Together in life, in family, in love, *now*.

Maria rose to meet him, Ellison's openmouthed kisses like washes of fire, Maria burning to ash beneath him.

She reached out to brush aside her fear, and found it dissolving under his heat and love, like dust motes over bluebonnets on a Texas spring breeze.

Tiger Striped

A Shifter Christmas Carol

Iron Master

The Last Warrior

Tiger's Daughter

Bear Facts

Stray Cat

Shifter Made ("Prequel" novella)

Stormwalker Series (w/a Allyson James)

Stormwalker

Firewalker

Shadow Walker

"Double Hexed"

Nightwalker

Dreamwalker

Dragon Bites

Wing Dancer

Shape Changer

(novella featuring Dylan)
The Last Warrior (Ben and Rhianne)
(Ben crosses over to other Shiftertowns)
Tiger's Daughter (Connor and Tiger-Girl)

Kendrick's Group
(Most cross over with Austin Shifters)
Lion Eyes (Seamus and Bree)
White Tiger (Kendrick and Addison)
Red Wolf (Jaycee and Dimitri)

Las Vegas Shifters
Wild Cat (Cassidy and Diego)
Mate Claimed (Eric and Iona)
Perfect Mate (Nell and Cormac)
Wild Wolf (Graham and Misty)
Iron Master (Stuart Reid and Peigi)
Bear Facts (Shane and Freya)
Stray Cat (Xav and Lindsay)

North Carolina Shifters
Mate Bond (Bowman and Kenzie.
Crossover with Las Vegas Shifters)

New Orleans Shifters
Midnight Wolf (Angus and Tamsin.
Crosses over with Austin Shifters and Zander)

Montana Shifters
Guardian's Mate (Zander and Rae)

Note: I include Zander with the Montana Shifters, because Rae is from the Montana Shiftertown, but Zander moves between all the groups. It's his way.

Check my website:

https://www.jenniferashley.com

for additions as I continue to explore all the Shiftertowns!

All my best,

Jennifer Ashley

ABOUT THE AUTHOR

New York Times bestselling and award-winning author Jennifer Ashley has more than 120 published novels and novellas in mystery, romance, historical fiction, and urban fantasy under the names Jennifer Ashley, Allyson James, and Ashley Gardner. Jennifer's books have been translated into more than a dozen languages and have earned starred reviews in *Publisher's Weekly* and *Booklist*. When she isn't writing, Jennifer enjoys playing music (guitar, piano, flute), reading, hiking, cooking, and building dollhouse miniatures.

More about Jennifer's books can be found at

http://www.jenniferashley.com

To keep up to date on her new releases, join her newsletter here:

http://eepurl.com/47kLL